He had to have her.

And then he must walk away, as she had walked out on him. OK, he was talking stubborn Neapolitan pride here—but until he felt justice had been done he wouldn't be able to put the past behind him.

Slowly he turned around. She was slipping her feet into a pair of very feminine sandals. He swallowed, remembering how he'd used to coax off her shoes very slowly and... Hastily he closed his mind to what had happened next. He needed to stay in control every step of the way. 'I have a suggestion.' He spoke calmly. 'You come to my hotel and stay for the week. It's an exclusive hide-away for VIPs and celebrities...'

'Sounds terrific...but who's paying?' Ellen asked cautiously.

You are, he wanted to say. But not in the way she might think!

Childhood in Portsmouth meant grubby knees, flying pigtails and happiness for **Sara Wood**. Poverty drove her from typist and seaside landlady to teacher, till writing finally gave her the freedom her Romany blood craved. Happily married, she has two handsome sons: Richard is calm, dependable, drives tankers; Simon is a roamer—silversmith, roofer, welder—always with beautiful girls. Sara lives in the Cornish countryside. Her glamorous writing life alternates with her passion for gardening which allows her to be carefree and grubby again!

Recent titles by the same author:

EXPECTANT MISTRESS
TEMPORARY PARENTS

A HUSBAND'S VENDETTA

BY
SARA WOOD

All the characters in this book have no existence outside the imagination of the author, and have no relation whatsoever to anyone bearing the same name or names. They are not even distantly inspired by any individual known or unknown to the author, and all the incidents are pure invention.

First published in Great Britain 1999
Harlequin Mills & Boon Limited,
Eton House, 18-24 Paradise Road, Richmond, Surrey TW9 1SR

© Sara Wood 1999

ISBN 0 263 81495 5

Set in Times Roman 10½ on 11 pt.
01-9903 55717 C1

Printed and bound in Norway
by AIT Trondheim AS, Trondheim

CHAPTER ONE

IT WAS a Wednesday, so they were talking English.
Although his daughter had a good grasp of the language,
Luciano chose his words carefully as he admired the picture she had presented to him.

'Thank you, sweetheart! How handsome I am!' he marvelled, with a theatrical astonishment calculated to make
her laugh.

Gemma obliged with a burst of giggles. Shyly she drew
his attention to the figure of a woman in the doorway of
a house she'd drawn. Although he smiled and nodded
approvingly, he felt his stomach churn. Poor kid. She
wanted a mother. Definitely not her own mother—they
both loathed her—but a new one. Much to his dismay,
Gemma had begun to suggest potential candidates almost
daily, and her desperation was unnerving.

Luc's finely shaped mouth dived down at the corners.
Living with Gemma was like being in an emotional minefield.

'Look. I put the picture by my heart,' he said, forcing
a cheerful tone.

Gemma's eyes glowed with pleasure when he slipped
the drawing into the inside pocket of his finely tailored
suit and she happily turned her attention to her ice cream.
Luc smiled and relaxed a little. He'd bought it as an after-school treat—and a downright bribe.

Sipping his espresso at the table of their favourite café,
he allowed his mind to drift. Idly he watched the tourists
and celebrities wander through Capri's elegant little
square as they explored the delights of the ultra-chic island. He felt a flash of fierce pride that many of them

5

would have travelled over on one of his hydrofoils, either from Naples or Sorrento on the Italian coast.

In the morning he'd be travelling to Naples on his way to England, an urgent trip to check out a new venture. Edgily he squared his broad shoulders, knowing he must tell Gemma—but dreading her reaction. Emotional minefields had a habit of exploding, as he knew to his cost.

'This is nice,' he murmured, speaking slowly. Shamelessly he descended to yet more bribery. 'We will do this every day after school…' He hesitated, and took the plunge. 'After I come back from my trip to London tomorrow.'

He watched her whole body stiffen. She gazed stonily ahead, as if denying his existence, and his stomach muscles contracted. He'd seen that expression before. Gemma's English mother, Ellen, had produced it often, and it chilled him to the bone that his daughter had mastered it so well.

'*Olà*, look at me!' he urged gently, shaken by her icy stare.

'I want to come!' She virtually flung the words forcibly through her small white teeth.

For 'want', read *will*, he thought with a sigh. 'You hate England. Stay here with Maria,' he coaxed. 'She makes you laugh.'

But the mention of their friendly maid didn't do its usual trick. He could see hysteria in Gemma's eyes and it made him feel unusually helpless.

Now what? he wondered. Did he give in, or play the stern father? He'd always been particularly careful to ensure that his daughter didn't always have her own way. And yet… His heart softened at his daughter's sullen face. He couldn't be too strict on the child. She had good reason to feel insecure.

Her mother had abandoned her as a baby.

Moodily he pushed his sunglasses to the top of his head. Beneath the perfectly groomed, panther-sleek ex-

terior, a surge of murderous anger was sweeping through
him. Hatred for his estranged wife wiped the lazy smile
from his affectionate mouth and replaced it with a savage
snarl. Suddenly the sharp planes of his face and the
slightly sinister angle of his broken nose became strikingly prominent and the darker side of his nature surfaced.

Ellen. He muttered a heartfelt curse under his breath.
The woman had ruined the most precious person in his
life and turned her into a complex mass of neuroses. He
scowled, hoping with all his heart that his estranged wife
was in her own hell somewhere.

With an effort, he clawed back his composure, only the
steep angle of his pitch-black brows showing the strain
he was under. He pushed away his coffee, planning how
to win Gemma around quickly. Out of the corner of his
eye he could see that his mobile was flashing, announcing
that he had a bank of calls waiting.

'Sweetheart,' he began persuasively, his neatly mani-
cured forefinger turning her small, set face to his.

Perhaps mistakenly sensing surrender, she smiled like
an angel. The breath caught in his throat. Even in her
starched school pinafore she was the loveliest child he'd
ever seen. Tenderly he reached out and caressed her
creamy skin, admiring the symmetry of her face and the
luxuriance of her blonde hair...

So like her mother! A sense of dread spilled into him,
obliterating every ounce of fatherly pride and pleasure.
Maybe his Gemma had inherited all of Ellen's flaws.
Maybe she'd be selfish and spoilt and would use and
discard people too, as if they were worthless, broken toys!

Shadows darkened the inky depths of his eyes and pain
distorted the high arc of his mouth. Here was a sweet and
innocent child. He couldn't bear to think of her growing
up to be vindictive and cruel. Not his baby.

Somehow, he vowed with silent passion, he would
teach her to be kind and considerate and to think of others. She had to learn that life didn't revolve around her.

It pained him to deny her because he loved her more than anything in the world. But he had to steel himself to do so.

'I love you. You know that,' he began, kissing both of her peachy cheeks in reassurance.

She instantly rewarded him with a joyful hug. 'I love *you*, Papà!' she cried in triumph, clearly expecting victory.

Luc groaned inwardly. He was handling this badly! 'Listen. I am sorry, Gemma. You can't come,' he said, his eyes warmly adoring as he tried to soften the blow. 'You are a big girl of six and have started school—'

'No school!' she cried in alarm.

'Sweetheart, I can't look after you in England. I will be too busy working. *Occupato.* Understand?'

'Ellen!' she cried, wriggling in agitation. 'I go to Ellen!'

He froze, astounded by her suggestion. All her life she'd hated her mother. The last time he'd prepared Gemma for a visit to England, she'd cried all the way to the airport! What the hell was going on here?

'No, Gemma! You have school; I told you!' he said sternly, before he could stop himself.

Gemma flinched as if he'd hit her, and he winced too, kissing the top of her head in earnest apology and cursing Ellen for causing him to speak roughly to his child.

The woman brought out the worst in him. She'd ripped him apart by walking out. Taken his trust, his love, commitment, hopes and dreams... Dammit. It hurt to remember. He clenched his jaw hard.

He'd ruthlessly banished her from his thoughts. That was the only way he'd been able to cope. Ellen's rejection of Gemma had turned his child into an emotional mess and he'd never forgive Ellen for that.

Sometimes he burned to take his revenge. But he didn't want to be dragged down to Ellen's level again. Better to stay away, to keep his dignity and not go brawling in the gutter.

'Papà! Papà!'

Gemma was looking at his grim face nervously. Trembling, she flung herself into his lap and wrapped her arms tightly around his neck. To his dismay, she began to weep. Choked with emotion, he stroked her incredible mass of corn-coloured curls and kissed her small forehead.

'I am going for three days, no more. Three days. Very quick!'

Gemma refused to be consoled and the tears continued to cascade down her face. Hell, he thought bleakly, it was tough being the only parent. Every time he left home for a few days he went on a guilt trip too. Yet he had to make a living.

And the purpose of this trip was special, something he'd been working for ever since Ellen's father had sacked him for being presumptuous enough to love his daughter. Somehow he must convince Gemma that he had to go.

With a heavy heart, he rose, while Gemma clung to him like a limpet. Deftly he slipped a few lire notes beneath his saucer and negotiated the crowded tables. People stared when he went by, his dark and handsome head bent to the small fair one, his achingly sensual mouth close to the child's pale cheek as he spoke in low, lilting murmurs.

Luc was oblivious of everyone and strode purposefully through the medieval arch which led from La Piazzetta into the narrow, cobbled street of Via Vittorio Emanuele.

Crying and pleading at the same time, she began to hyperventilate. Appalled that her distress was quite out of all proportion, Luc sat on a wall opposite a row of designer boutiques and cuddled her, hating Ellen with all his heart, wanting to wound her as he and Gemma had been wounded.

After a moment or two, he found it impossible to stand her misery any longer. The child had suffered enough and so had he.

'All right. You can come. I will ask your mother,' he said, defeated by her sobs and the inconstancy of the whole damn female race. Gemma's body relaxed, but she still clung to him like a drowning man to a rock.

He felt very worried about her. On the long walk home he tried to work out why she had become so possessive. Every morning, since starting school a month ago, she'd complained of pains in her stomach, but nothing was physically wrong and the teachers had said she was a model pupil. Why, then, was she having nightmares?

He racked his brains. Something to do with Ellen... Gemma's insecurity... The answer came to him in a blinding flash. She might be afraid that he wouldn't be there when she got home.

His eyes blazed with pain and anger. Poor, frightened little scrap! Seething with suppressed fury, he pushed open the huge iron gates of his villa. It perched high on wooded slopes above the sea and normally the view gave him a sense of joy. Today he was indifferent to it.

He had decisions to make. Grimly he strode down broad steps shaded by tall pines and hibiscus shrubs, re-shaping his life as he went with ruthless zeal. Gemma must be protected and reassured at all costs. This must be his last business trip abroad.

The lines on his brow smoothed out. He'd make use of Ellen as a babysitter on this brief and final trip because it suited him. Then he'd tell her point-blank that she'd never see his daughter again.

The flat door was warped. She'd forgotten this. With a grimace, Ellen dragged it open as far as it would go and sucked in her breath so that she could do a kind of vertical limbo through it, simultaneously thanking her lucky stars that poverty had made her slim.

Once in the room, she blinked in momentary confusion. She'd only moved in a few days ago and everything still seemed strange and new.

'New!'

She giggled, and her spontaneous peal of laughter rang around the under-furnished room. Everything in the flat, she mused, her eyes brimming with merriment—the vile yellow wallpaper and lino the colour of hippo mud included—must be coming up for its quarter century.

'You too, ducky,' she reminded herself drily.

Almost twenty-five and a daughter without parents. Married, but minus a husband. A mother without the love of her child.

She stopped herself hastily. There she went again! That was her old, maudlin way of thinking. Being sorry for herself wouldn't change her age or marital status. It wouldn't make her part of a happy family or bring her daughter back.

Ellen bolted the door firmly, as if she were finally closing it on the nightmare of her past. She'd resolved to stop wishing her life away and intended to enjoy each day to the full. New job, new flat, new *her*. Life was on the up and she was happier now than she'd been for a long time.

Heading cheerfully for the shower, she clambered out of her clothes as she went. Habit made her gather them up and fold them neatly on a chair.

It wasn't habit, however, which made her slip on a simple top and body-hugging skirt fifteen minutes later. *That* was part of the conscious attempt to re-create herself. She loved her new clothes and felt liberated in them— which was exactly the attitude she was aiming for.

Sandwich in mouth, mug of tea to hand, Ellen flopped, exhausted, on the bed-settee and hooked her bare legs over its shabby brown back.

'Oh, bliss, oh, rapture!' she murmured in exaggerated appreciation, through a mouthful of wholewheat and organic cheddar. 'Best part of the day!'

She slipped one smooth ankle over the other and smiled with some affection at the familiar roughness of uncut moquette on the backs of her legs. In the last six ghastly years she'd moved five times. And there'd been a tatty fox-brown sofa with wooden arms in every single flat she'd occupied!

This version won the prize for discomfort, with two twanging springs and an itchy patch beneath her back, where her top had ridden up. She squirmed ineffectually.

She'd have to stir herself. Her evening job depended on her having a flawless skin—but if she stayed put much longer she'd turn up with all the symptoms of some infectious disease across her back! She smiled to think of the problems that would cause.

Stretching out a long, creamy arm, she captured a sagging cushion and pushed it into the supple arch of her spine. Now she could display her body all evening without anyone calling in the public health authorities and bleating that she had chickenpox!

Satisfied, she reached for the mug and balanced it on the washboard-flatness of her Lycra-covered abdomen. And she thought of her daughter, as she often did, smiling gently at the intensely vivid image of a curly-headed child on the floor and toys strewn all around. Fish fingers and baked beans. Plastic ponies and surreal dolls in bubble-gum-pink net and flashing neon earrings.

Recklessly she added a dark, heartbreakingly handsome man, lounging companionably with her on the sofa, an arm looped around her shoulders as they watched their child.

And, perfectly well aware that this was an unrealistic and downright stupid dream, which would give her grief if she allowed it to continue, she commanded it to vanish, turning her mind instead to safer, more mundane pleasures.

'Heaven is hot, sweet tea after a long, hard day,' she declared happily to the empty room, letting the exhaustion seep wonderfully away into the brown moquette. 'Who needs silk knickers and Lapsang Souchong in bone china cups?' She waved her mug—decorated with frolicking wart-hogs—in a toast to simplicity.

Without a scrap of regret, she thought of the pretentious mansion in Devon where she'd been brought up. The servants. Her overbearing father—who'd disowned her when she said she was going to marry one of his lorry drivers—and who felt awkward in his new surroundings like many self-made men. She thought sadly of her nervous mother, equally out of her depth and totally under her father's thumb. Ellen mused that they probably weren't as happy as she was.

It was odd how dramatically her life had changed. And she'd changed most of all. Ellen ruefully smoothed a hand over her cropped hair. Once she'd had a luxuriant mass of curls. It had always been her one big vanity. But not any more.

Luc had liked her to wear it loose. He'd adored it. Had loved to bury his nose in its perfumed strands or thread his fingers through the tumbling curls. But those moments were over for ever. A little wistfully her fingers sought the short hairs curving into the nape of her neck.

With a shrug, she dismissed the consequences of her marriage break-up, consigning them to the bin of bad experiences. And, feeling wonderfully in control of her life at last, she drank her tea and put down the mug with a sigh of deep pleasure.

Ahead lay half an hour of sheer and richly deserved self-indulgence. One bar of chocolate, to be devoured nibble by nibble; one zany-looking magazine to be read, which had been lent to her by one of the girls at work. She smiled, amused by her eager anticipation of such ordinary things. Was she a mover and shaker or what!

Thoughtfully she gave her bare toes a little wiggle. After that half-hour of wild excitement, it was back to her evening job. It had started by accident. She'd taken up art as a therapy during the long illness which had followed Gemma's birth. Then one day the life model had announced that she was going abroad—and Ellen had temporarily taken her place, nervously stipulating that she'd never pose in the nude.

Something had happened when she'd been posing, though. Inexplicably, she'd acquired a confidence in herself again. Dear, kind Paul—the art teacher—had respected her shyness, and the class was so supportive that she felt able to trust them. Now she felt secure enough to expose a little more of her body, knowing that everyone there was interested only in reproducing muscle depth and structure. These people were her friends too, and she loved seeing them.

Luc, of course, would never understand this. He'd probably forbid her from ever seeing Gemma again. Thank God he never came within five miles of her! Giving a heartfelt grunt, she banished stray breadcrumbs from her stomach. Luc always sent his devoted PA to deliver and collect Gemma on the regulation four times a year she came to visit.

Ellen's skin tightened like wafer-thin paper over her slanting Garbo cheekbones, her mood sobering despite her resolution. Luc shunned her because he couldn't bear to set eyes on her, as if she were some vile kind of Gorgon. But then she'd committed the ultimate sin of walking out on him, their marriage and their six-month-old baby. No one did that to an Italian male and came off lightly.

'Oh, *hell*!' she muttered in exasperation.

For, despite all her high-flown intentions, she was reliving it all now and quivering like a leaf, desperately fighting down the nausea which always came with the unendurable memories.

Ellen stared blindly into space, wondering if she would ever get over what had happened, if one day the pain would become just a dull ache and then vanish completely. As much as she tried to forget, and to look to the future, some days she thought that she couldn't stand the situation any longer. There were times when she felt it would be better never to see Gemma at all.

Ellen let out a long, unhappy sigh. Sometimes it was as if she were living on a perpetual white-knuckle ride. Every time she got her life back together again and stopped crying into her pillow, Gemma's next visit hove into sight. And she, Ellen, had to go through the mill all over again.

Well, a short while ago she'd decided that she'd had enough. Living in the past was getting her nowhere. Grab happiness where she could, enjoy each moment—that was to be her rule. She had to protect herself from negative thoughts.

She pulled the cushion from behind her back and cuddled it. No wonder absent fathers sometimes chose not to retain their visiting rights, she thought sadly. Part-time parenting was a desperately painful thing to do. Her heart was in shreds every time Gemma left.

And everything became magnified out of all proportion. How could you act naturally when you desperately wanted everything to be perfect? Who could shrug off small organisational hiccups like stair-rod rain on the day you'd planned a picnic? Or when your child looked with contempt at a toy you'd spent hours searching for and couldn't even afford?

Feeling aggrieved, she drew her knees up to her chest, hating Luc with all her heart, angry with him for not supporting her when she'd needed him so badly after Gemma's birth. He'd thought the worst of her. And so she'd lost her child.

For the millionth time, Ellen tried to persuade herself to do the sensible thing: to call Luc and suggest Gemma stopped visiting at all. The kiddie hated coming to England. She hated the language, the weather, the food, and the insularity of everyone...

Nothing Ellen ever did could shift the boredom and resentment which showed in every line of Gemma's small body. Oh, yes. She knew what she ought to do. But she couldn't bring herself to make that final break because she loved her daughter desperately.

Tears sneaked up on her unawares and began to trickle into her hair, tracking their way over her temples in hot, sticky rivulets. It was natural that Gemma would find separation from her father hard to bear. Natural that she should be scared in a strange country and would reject everything connected with it.

And so Ellen had built a wall of protection around herself. It was the only way she'd coped with the heartbreaking goodbyes. The result was that the two of them remained politely suffering strangers.

There were no hugs, no spontaneous laughter and no kisses. She'd seen other women with their children and had ached to be loved so. But the bond had never been made between them.

Sitting up, she gazed in blurred sentimentality at the most recent photo of Gemma. And lovingly, unable to caress her child, she stroked its shiny surface instead. Then she picked up the photo from the table beside the sofa and held it to the softness of her breast.

This was what she was reduced to. Nursing a bit of glossy paper. Pathetic. Oh, Luc, she reflected, her eyes full of sorrow, if only we'd met now, and not seven years ago!

'Telephone!'

She groaned at her landlord's yell. Impatiently he began to pound on her door. 'Who is it?' she called irritably, expecting any minute to see his big hairy hand punching a hole in the thin plywood.

'Some bloke for you!' bellowed Cyril.

She heaved a sigh. It often was. Men seemed to be fascinated by her indifference to them and would never take 'no' for an answer until they'd heard it several times.

But there had been no man in her life since Luc. She'd been hurt too badly. And, despite her new confidence, she wasn't ready to risk a new relationship. Some time in the future, perhaps. Not now.

'OK. Coming!'

Reluctantly she replaced the school photo. Her daughter was growing up fast—without her. Ellen drew in a ragged breath and scrubbed her eyes with a handkerchief. Tough. That was her lot. Some people had worse burdens.

Fiercely counting her blessings, she stood up, rearranged her face into an expression of polite enquiry and yanked her skirt snugly into place as her fluid stride took her quickly across the poky little room and she began her struggle with the door.

'Push!' she yelled.

Cyril leant his considerable body-weight against the door, and after a while they managed to drag it open. 'Sounded urgent,' he wheezed, in his sleazy manner.

As always, he did his best to remove her clothes by will-power alone, leering eagerly at her bra-less top and her bare legs and feet. Ellen gave him a cool and level stare.

'Then I suggest you move out of my way so I can get to the phone quickly,' she said briskly, determined not to squeeze past his sweating bulk on the narrow landing.

He smirked, clearly wanting her to do just that. Ellen hardened her eyes till they gleamed like flint, folded her arms and took a purposeful step forward. 'Move,' she said, sweetness laced with steel. 'Or delicate parts of your person and my knee will become painfully acquainted.'

He stepped aside faster than she would have thought possible. With her body jarring on every angry thump of her bare heels, she stalked to the phone.

Girl power 1, vile old man 0! She blessed the girls in the supermarket where she worked during the day. It was they who'd taught her how to deal with male harassment and had coaxed her back into the real world again.

'Italian bloke. Loo-charno,' offered Cyril grumpily.

Luciano! Her stomach and heart did a few high jumps. Incredulously, she saw that her hands had begun to shake at the prospect of talking to him. Since their parting they'd only spoken through intermediaries.

Suddenly, into her head came the unforgettable sound of his liquid, seductive voice which made everything he said sound lyrical and sensual—even the reading of a shopping list. She'd adored listening to him. Often she'd coaxed him to talk about his life in Naples purely to hear him speak.

Her bones seemed to flow like warm treacle in anticipation. 'OK. Thanks,' she said, trying to get them back to their normal state. What a stupid reaction!

And then it dawned on her why he must be calling. *Gemma!* Something must be wrong! Petrified, she froze, staring at the dangling receiver and listening in dismay to the violent bumping of her heart.

Cyril's hot breath drifted moistly over the long sweep of her exposed neck, sending shivers down her back. 'Men are always calling you!' he complained loudly. 'I'm fed up with answering the phone and taking messages.'

'You're exaggerating! This,' she snapped, grabbing the receiver from him and covering the mouthpiece as a precaution, 'is probably my husband.' Wisely she omitted the word 'estranged'. 'A bad-tempered and possessive man, topping six foot and with the biceps of an ox,' she invented in a rush, desperate to get rid of her landlord.

To her relief, Cyril took the heavy hint. In the ensuing silence, she could hear Luc impatiently calling her name. Her breathing quickened. She knew he wouldn't have rung unless it was a real emergency. Blocking her mind to several nightmare scenarios, she made herself speak.

'I'm here,' she said, fear making her voice catch breathily in her throat. 'Is it Gemma? Is she all right? What—?'

'She's fine,' he broke in.

'Thank goodness!'

Ellen subsided in relief and then registered that he didn't sound liquid or seductive at all. In fact he seemed positively furious, his voice harsh and rasping.

'Who was that man I spoke to?' he demanded.

Ellen blinked, her anxiety forgotten. 'Nobody you need to know about!' she replied in stunned surprise.

'I do. So stop stalling and tell me!' Luc ordered.

'What on earth for?' she countered, bristling at his arrogant manner.

'Because,' he said tightly, 'he was panting.'

In exasperation she racked her brains to understand why that should annoy him so much, but couldn't think of any explanation. 'Probably. He often does,' she agreed, like a mother humouring a child.

Luc inhaled deeply, as if she'd said something inflammatory. 'Because he suffers from asthma,' he queried cuttingly, 'or because I interrupted something intimate?'

She burst out laughing. 'Oh, Luc, if you only knew!' she spluttered.

Luc growled something rude under his breath, her laughter doing little for his bad temper. 'I don't. I'm trying to find out why you took so long to answer.'

Her laughter faded away and her jaw dropped open in amazement. 'What is this? Working for the KGB, are you?' she asked crossly.

'I want to know,' he said, giving each word heavy emphasis.

Ellen glared, wishing fervently that her contempt could be conveyed down the line. Wasn't it just typical that Luc's first thought was to imagine the worst of her? And who the hell did he think he was, asking about her private life?

'I took a while to answer the phone because my door was stuck,' she said coolly.

'Is that so?'

She felt her hackles rising. She'd told the truth. The

jammed door had delayed her. But he didn't believe her. He never believed her.

'Look, the man lives here. He has every right to answer the phone. Do you have a problem with that?' she asked, upping the count of frost particles in her voice.

From his silence, it seemed he did, though again she couldn't understand why. And then she remembered that he didn't know she lived in a block of flats. He'd assumed that Cyril had answered the phone because they lived *together*. She frowned. Surely there was nothing wrong with that, even if it were true?

'You didn't tell me you had a lover.'

'No, I didn't,' she agreed.

Judging by the heavy breathing at Luc's end, either he was developing asthma, had just made love himself, or her non-replies were driving him crazy. She grinned to herself, pleased with the fact that she wasn't melting all over the floor in response to Luc's voice—or quivering with nerves from his intimidation.

'So. You omit to tell me something that could affect Gemma. Could your relationship with this man be responsible for her distress last time she visited you?' he rapped out, for all the world, Ellen thought in amazement, like a prosecutor on a murder case!

'Absolutely not! I've no idea what upset her,' she answered confidently.

'Unfortunately I *can* imagine,' Luc muttered. 'Gemma must have been in the way. You had other things on your mind.'

Displeasure and disgust riddled every word. She had an instant and compelling image of him, as clear as if he stood in front of her. Painfully she saw the anger blazing in his smouldering dark eyes, that anger as volatile as a volcano. But then he came from Naples, which was close to Vesuvius, and he'd told her once that people there tended to live each moment to its fullest, loving and hating with intense passion.

That was Luc. Her last memory of him was frozen in that moment when his emotions had erupted and destroyed her. It was frightening how a man could turn from lover to tyrant in a matter of weeks.

God, she'd loved him! Every glorious, gorgeous inch. The glossy black hair, the olive skin and ruinously exotic cheekbones... Ellen groaned. Life was springing into her sexually slumbering body now: fierce, urgent and utterly pointless.

Why was she doing this to herself? Why torment herself with memories of earth-shattering sex, of days in bed, hours talking, sitting silently and just gazing into each other's eyes? A searing ache slashed at her like a lightning bolt from her breast to the apex of her loins, and she uttered a shuddering gasp of dismay.

'What the devil is going on now?' Luc demanded furiously.

'Nothing!' she mumbled. But that was untrue. There was a battle raging between her brain and her hormones. 'Am I forbidden to breathe in and out now?'

'If that was breathing, your lungs need attention,' he said scathingly. 'Get rid of the boyfriend! Tell him to stop playing around! I refuse to talk to you while he whispers sweet nothings—and does God knows what—!'

'Are you mad?' she broke in, astounded by his vehemence. 'Why are you making such an issue of this? You don't own me body and soul any more! I might have been making mad, passionate love on the kitchen table; you might have interrupted me with my lover,' she rampaged on, deciding to let Luc stew. 'But what's that to you? It's not any of your business what I get up to!'

'Unfortunately it is!' he insisted. 'Your morals are very much my business. I have to protect my daughter.'

'From what?'

'You! And your lovers. I won't have Gemma mixing with people of dubious character. I don't want her watching one man after another pawing you—!'

'Oh, for goodness' sake, give me some credit!' she snorted. 'What do you think I do when she comes to stay?' she asked indignantly. 'Take her out for a lesson in needle techniques with a bunch of drug addicts? Read the kiddies' Bedtime Kama Sutra? Bed three men a night?' she suggested, so angry that her imagination was overheating.

'How the devil would I know?' he flung back. 'You always wanted freedom from responsibility. And you had one hell of a sex drive—'

'God, Luc!' she fumed, her disgust growing with every word he uttered. This wasn't funny any more. *He'd* woken her desire. She'd responded only to him. How could he not realise that? She wanted to punch him on the nose for being so dense. 'You've built up a nasty little picture of me in your head, haven't you? You really think I'm stupid, selfish and irresponsible—'

'You said it. And, remember, you proved it.' He let the accusation lie there in a heavy silence which it was beneath her pride to break. She heard him give a heavy sigh of defeat. 'Now what?' he muttered, as if to himself. 'I clearly can't trust you.'

She felt a small pang, knowing that it must be hard for him to surrender Gemma to someone he thought was utterly irresponsible.

'I understand why you worry,' she said, with marginally more sympathy. 'I see why you were quizzing me. But I assure you that she's perfectly safe with me—'

'I would like to believe that. But… Oh, forget it. This is pointless—'

'No, it's not!' she cried quickly, scared that he'd cut her access time. She could have kicked herself for not telling him about Cyril straight away. But it was too late now. He'd never accept her explanation. 'You must know that I'd never do anything to upset or hurt her,' she said fervently.

'Is that so?' he bit. 'What do you call abandoning her,

then? Why ignore her needs—and why did you run away the minute motherhood didn't turn out to be all coochie-coos and dimpled cheeks?'

She couldn't speak. He'd struck her dumb with his cruelty.

'You can't answer, can you?' he said bitterly. 'God, I was a fool to imagine you'd change. I should have realised that you'd still be going your own sweet way and indulging your selfish needs with an over-active love life—'

Ellen interrupted him with a groan. She lifted her eyes to the ceiling in exasperation. What love life?

'Tell me about it!' she said wryly.

'I only know what I heard your lover say. It seems you're not even faithful to him,' Luc said coldly. 'Poor fool seemed to think I was another of your boyfriends. Is it any wonder that I despair of your morals? Do you know what it does to me, to imagine—' He broke off. Then he continued with a blistering passion. 'To imagine my daughter being exposed to the seamier side of life?'

Her teeth ground together hard. She seriously contemplated banging the phone down and ending this pointless conversation. He wasn't to know that men might pester her, but she kept her distance because as sure as hell she wasn't going to be hurt so badly again. Nor was she going to tell him. But she'd give as good as she got.

'So it's OK for you to take women-friends and Gemma skiing or lazing on beaches in the Caribbean,' she said, sweetly poisonous, 'but I have to live like a Carmelite nun?'

'I should be so lucky.' He grunted. 'If you did, at least I'd know Gemma would be cared for and protected.'

'She *is* cared for and protected when she's here!'

'Huh.' He sounded utterly unconvinced. 'What exactly did she tell you about our holidays?' he asked warily.

Ellen winced. He obviously had things to hide. 'Not a word. She never speaks about you. Or your home,' she replied, feeling suddenly mournful. 'I developed a roll of film for her when she was here in August.'

Seeing the holiday pictures had driven home some painful truths. Luc had no hang-ups about his shattered marriage. The photos had shown him with Gemma, laughing and fooling around and totally at ease with two gorgeous women. She made a face. Was there any other kind where Luc was concerned?

She'd pored over the snaps when Gemma had gone to bed. The intense happiness in her daughter's face had made her cry. She knew she could never have that effect on her child. It had been a terrible moment, one she'd never forget.

And it was bad enough that she couldn't afford to take her daughter anywhere exciting, let alone seeing her child being cuddled by a couple of Miss Worlds. One day, Miss World would become Miss Right.

And then Miss Right would gracefully take on the role of the second Mrs Luciano Maccari. Gemma would have a mother to tuck her up in bed and read stories... Hastily Ellen shut off that line of thought. It was an inevitable development but she wasn't ready for it yet.

As for Luc—he was a hypocrite! He saw nothing wrong in letting women paw him in front of his daughter, she thought indignantly. One of them had been sitting on his lap, the other had flung her arms around his neck and was kissing him on the cheek while he grinned in smug delight.

Yet he was condemning her for entertaining non-existent lovers! She steamed with the rank injustice of it. Justifiably aggrieved, hurting at the memory of those lovely women, she stood up for herself.

'Let's make a pact. You lead your own life,' she told him tightly, 'and I'll do what I damn well like with mine!'

'Not when my daughter's around, you won't!' he countered.

'She's mine too!'

'Barely!' he shot back

Ellen sucked in a painful breath. He was determined to inflict wounds. The brute.

'You hate not having control over everything that happens to her, don't you? For heaven's sake, Luc, don't carp. She's yours for most of the time. I only see her for one week, four times a year!'

'Ye-e-e-s.'

There was a significance in his hesitation and she blanched, fearing what would follow from that 'ye-e-e-s.' Nervously she said, 'Why did you ring?'

'It doesn't matter. I've changed my mind.'

Her jaw tightened ominously. He'd ruined her evening for nothing! 'Right,' she said tersely. 'Fascinating chat. Goodbye, Luc—'

'Wait...' There was a long and tense pause, as if he was trying to broach a difficult subject. And then he said in a tired voice, 'We need to meet up, Ellen.'

'No, we don't. Anyway, what happened to your declaration when you threw me out that you never wanted to see me again?'

'I said "need", not "want",' he drawled sardonically.

'It makes no difference. I'm not interested in seeing you.' But she couldn't stop her curiosity prompting her to add, 'Why on earth should we *need* to meet?'

'Things to talk about.'

'Like...what?' she asked guardedly, warning bells ringing in her head.

It could be about access. Or... She thought of the women in the photographs and the blonde one in particular, who'd been gazing adoringly at him as if he was the source of all life.

Perhaps he wanted a divorce. He wanted his freedom to remarry. Her heart swooped and dived as if she were inside an elevator.

'I'm not discussing it on the phone,' he replied stubbornly. 'This is something we need to do face to face. What are you doing this evening?'

Her mouth dropped open in amazement. 'This...! Oh, my God! You—you're in *England*?' she croaked, her throat as dry as dust.

No. She couldn't see him. She was getting stage fright at the very thought. He'd talk about the woman he loved and his eyes would melt with love and she'd be dying inside.

'Sudden business came up.'

'Yes, well, I'm working, so put your comments in writing,' she told him flatly.

'Working...tonight?'

Stung by the wealth of suggestion in the way he'd said that, she primmed her mouth and then said with laboured patience, 'Relax, Luc. I'm not patrolling the back alleys of Southwark in fishnet stockings and very little else!'

'I'm relieved to hear it,' he bit, and she wondered what had happened to his wonderful sense of humour. 'Did Daddy find you a lucrative job?' he murmured insolently.

She sniffed. As if she needed help from anyone! 'I found my own. Your sidekick Donatello must have told you I don't live with my parents any more.'

'Got thrown out for impossible behaviour?'

'Got sick and tired of being pushed around by yet another bossy man!' she retorted hotly.

Luc grunted. 'What *are* you doing to earn your living, then?'

'I stack shelves in the local supermarket during the day and...' She chickened out. She couldn't tell him about her evening job! Being economical with the truth, she said, 'Three times a week I work at the community centre in the evenings. That's where I'm going tonight.'

There was a long pause. A hectic colour flushed her neck and face and she was glad he couldn't see it. He wouldn't think much of her progress since she'd left him.

He wasn't to know she'd been fighting depression for more than five years.

He'd never enquired after her welfare. The break had been brutally clean. She'd refused his offer of money and he'd washed his hands of her. Out of sight, out of mind.

'A...supermarket.' His disapproval was plain to hear.

'I love it,' she told him honestly, springing to her own defence. It was the first step of her career. One day she'd manage the store. Then—who knows?

'Stacking...*shelves*?'

She permitted herself a smile at his amazement. 'Oh, you know me,' she said sarcastically. 'All fun and no responsibility.'

'Sounds about right,' he agreed sourly, not recognising that he was being teased.

She raised her eyes to the ceiling in exasperation and gave up on him. 'I enjoy it there. It's like being part of a big family. We have a great time.'

In the pause which followed, Ellen thought sadly of her own dysfunctional family. And of Luc's doting widowed mother, who'd believed no one, absolutely no one, short of a canonised female saint, would have made a suitable wife for her beloved only son. His mother was dead now. Gemma must be his only blood relative, she mused.

'I'm glad you've found work that matches your skills,' Luc said rudely. 'Now. Tonight. What time do you start work?'

'Seven-thirty.' Her hand shook, and she glared at it for being so stupid. 'But I'm not seeing you—'

'You must. We'll meet beforehand.' He stated this in the confident, macho tone which had once made her feel cherished and protected. Now it irritated her beyond belief. 'Where? Your house?'

She frowned, hating to be pushed around. Inviting Luc to her flat was the last thing she wanted. She'd always met Gemma and Luc's PA, Donatello, at a local café to protect her privacy. She'd been afraid that Luc would stop Gemma visiting her if he knew how unsuitable her flat was.

'Why can't you get it into your head that I don't want to see you at all?' she complained crossly. 'You're a part of my past I'd rather stick in a sack and bury ten feet under.'

'That goes for me too. Do you think I want to see you? You're not exactly my favourite pin-up. But it's important,' he retorted. Ellen grumpily recognised that there must be a team of wild horses dragging him kicking and screaming in her direction. 'This is about Gemma. About you.'

She went cold. That sounded ominous. Her knees seemed to be giving out and she leaned heavily against the peeling wall. 'But can't we—?'

'This must be settled. Choose somewhere public,' he went on relentlessly, riding roughshod over her feeble objection. 'I only want ten minutes of your time.' His tone had become irascible. But then she wasn't fitting into his plans, was she? 'Surely you can grant me that, for the sake of my daughter's well-being?'

His, not *our*, daughter. Yes, she thought, that was how it was—and he meant to divorce her and demand that she surrender her access rights. An overwhelming sense of defeat enveloped her. Clearly—and understandably, considering the last time Gemma had visited her—he wasn't happy with even the limited access which the courts had granted her.

Crunch time. Well, she'd known it would come one day. She inhaled slowly, steadying her nerves. Before he broached the subject she would speak to him herself, tell him that she would relinquish what she'd fought so hard for. Seeing her own child grow up.

She drew in a long, shaky breath. She wanted to be the one who called things to a halt, not him. It was a matter of pride, of self-respect and of taking her own life in her hands.

Every fibre of her body shrank from what she must do. And yet, in her heart of hearts, she knew that Gemma didn't deserve to be dragged away from the home and father she adored and dumped on a mother she didn't love.

No, worse than that, a mother who frightened her. Ellen's eyes became filmed with a misty silver. What did the child fear?

The last time Gemma had come, she'd clung to Donatello as if Ellen were a hungry witch on the look-out for a child to fling into her stewpot. The entire visit had been a disaster. Gemma's silences, inexplicable terror and quiet, desperate sobbing at night had tortured Ellen so much that she'd phoned Donatello and begged him to rescue the little girl before three days had gone by.

Like it or not, she had to face facts. Once and for all, for the sake of her child, she had to forget her own needs. Gemma mustn't suffer any more.

Oh, God! she thought bleakly. A second sacrifice!

But it would make Gemma happy. That was all she wanted. And, despite the heaviness of her heart, she felt a little comfort in that.

Quickly, in case in a moment of weakness she changed her mind, she said, 'If I must, I must. There's a café in Lancaster Street by the tube station. Be there at seven.' And she cut the connection before he could suggest anything different.

Numb with the enormity of what she was about to do, she stood motionless by the phone, recovering her equilibrium. Or at least trying to. It seemed to have wandered off somewhere, leaving her floundering in a dark abyss.

It came to her then. Something which briefly eclipsed her thoughts of Gemma.

She was to meet Luc. After all this time.

A strange sensation filled her entire body. Ellen tried

to identify it and failed. Nor could she understand why adrenaline should have leapt through her like wildfire and put her into overdrive.

She was shaking like a leaf. And yet she was burning, too, with a weird excitement, her heart thudding like crazy.

Luc. The man she'd given everything to. Heart, soul, mind, body. And she'd surrendered her child to him, too.

Aching with the memories, she bit her lip till it hurt. She could be strong—she'd proved that. She wouldn't let him destroy her again. If he'd found happiness then good for him. Gemma would have a new mother...

Full of misery, she swallowed and concentrated fiercely on overcoming her near-hysteria. Gemma came first. Once again she'd do what was best for her child. And then she'd face the future square on.

A tear fell unexpectedly from her eye, and she moodily licked it up with the tip of her tongue before drawing herself erect. Courage, she told herself. Be calm.

Her shaking hands went instinctively to her heart. Pale, feeling bruised from tension, she prepared herself mentally for the worst. Tonight she would know if she had truly conquered her inner demons.

CHAPTER TWO

THE light in the hall went out and she tried not to see it as an omen. It was on a time clock to save Cyril money, and she hated the meanness that left her, old Mr Baker and Sally and her petrified children fumbling around in the pitch dark.

The damp-smelling blackness of the hall made her shiver. She hurried back to her flat. The door was stuck open and wouldn't budge. That was all she needed! She struggled in mounting fury with it and eventually dragged it shut.

A sense of panic skittered through her mind. Life was crowding in on her again, making difficulties. And she had to admit that she was scared of her ability to cope if too many things went wrong. A groan escaped her dry lips at the horror of losing control again and sinking into the black depths of suicidal despair. No. That mustn't happen.

'Help me, help me!' she whispered, forcing the words through her teeth.

As she walked shakily into the room, she caught a glimpse of her white and strained face in the mirror above the mantelpiece. She looked awful. Huge smudged eyes filled with misery. Sullen, down-turned mouth. Grimly she willed her spirits to rise.

Luc. She was seeing Luc after an eternity. He'd be…twenty-eight now. What would he think of her?! She took herself back to their first meeting. She'd been storming along the A38 near her home, in an attempt to walk off her fury after yet another row with her tyrannical and dogmatic father. She'd infuriated him by refusing to encourage the attentions of the limp, insufferably smug son of their wealthy neighbour. Her father had had ambitions for her. Most of them boiled down to seeing her married to a wealthy, influential man.

As she'd stomped along, steaming at her father's accusations of her wilfulness, ingratitude and downright stubborn stupidity, it had begun to rain in torrents, drenching her beautiful silk Bellini suit in seconds. No wonder Luc had stopped his lorry! He must have thought he was hallucinating, especially when she accepted his offer of a lift, slipped off her gorgeous Italian shoes, wriggled her expensive skirt up to her thighs and clambered up the high steps into the cab.

'I don't care where you're going,' she'd said grimly, not looking at him, not even aware that she'd picked an Adonis. 'Just drive me somewhere dry where I can fume for a while!'

That was then. And now…she saw a completely different woman. One who'd been to hell and back, grown wiser, more wary, more grateful for small mercies.

Her mind cleared, her soft, unhappy mouth grew firmer and she straightened, proud of how she'd survived, telling herself to be content with the person she'd become. When she'd left him she'd been scrawny and unhealthy-looking in a baggy old jumper and dowdy skirt, a walking scarecrow who'd forgotten what life and laughter were like.

She felt a hollow sensation in her stomach thinking of that ghastly moment when she'd found herself on the pavement outside their little house. What kind of mother left her child? A Class One cow, of course. She gave an involuntary shudder, her eyes as dark and shiny as rain-battered slate.

It hadn't occurred to Luc that there might be a powerful explanation for such unusual behaviour. He'd believed that she didn't love Gemma. Far from it. She'd put her daughter before her own needs. Always had, always would.

The birth had been awful. Her baby had been two weeks overdue and she'd been induced. The drugs had given her a protracted and painful labour and had left her in shock. It had been nearly a year before post-traumatic stress had been diagnosed and she'd begun treatment.

At the time, though, Luc had had no idea that her decision to leave was instinctive, to save Gemma's life. The greatest sacrifice she could make.

No. He hadn't even paused to think. Ellen let out a small sigh. They hadn't known one another very well. It had been a whirlwind courtship of fun and passion, and her reckless, impulsive behaviour in urging him to run away with her to London had contributed to the wrong impression he'd formed of her when she couldn't bond with her baby.

'What the hell are you doing?' he'd demanded, when he'd come home and found her case in the hall—and Gemma yelling her head off in the tiny sitting room beyond.

'Going.' It was all she could manage. A huge lump of emotion was blocking her throat. She desperately wanted to take Gemma in her arms. But didn't dare.

He gave an impatient snort of disbelief and pushed past her, grabbing the nappy sack and crouching on the carpet beside his screaming daughter. Confused, she watched from the doorway as he undid Gemma's rompers.

'God!' he said in disgust. 'She's soaking! What do you do all day? This place is a tip!'

'I...did change her, not long ago! Today?' She found it hard to think, her mind fuddled. 'I went shopping.'

Nervously she indicated a pile of bags full of clothes for herself which she didn't need and would never wear. And she didn't even know why she'd gone out, let alone bought the stuff. Absurd.

'Shopping!' he exploded. 'We're in debt, Ellen! I'm working all hours to pay just the interest! Why do you do this to me? Gemma's your priority, not yourself. You could have picked her up! Seen to her!'

No. No, she couldn't. She had to keep away and overcome that awful urge to grab Gemma and fling her across the room. No one understood. The doctor had put her on sedatives and implied that she was behaving like a spoilt child. Perhaps he'd even said as much to Luc!

After the birth Luc had been puzzled and then annoyed by her lack of interest in Gemma, but she was helpless in the face of the overwhelming fear that she would harm her child, and she was capable of focusing only on that one, overriding primitive instinct to protect her baby.

'I have to go!' she croaked, trembling and as limp as a rag doll.

He shot her a quick glance, his eyes narrowing as they searched hers. 'Where? We don't know anyone around here. Do you mean,' he asked tightly, 'that you're off to visit your parents? They're actually speaking to you again?'

Ellen licked her lips, her eyes hollow from night after night without sleep. 'I'm…leaving you.'

His shoulders rose and fell several times before he spoke. By that time Gemma had been deftly cleaned, dried and dressed again, and was tucked over her father's shoulder and whimpering quietly.

'What have I done?' he asked in a low tone. But despite his attempt at control, his voice was shaken.

'Nothing. It's me. I can't stay!' she blurted out. 'I can't stand it any longer.'

'It? Do you mean Gemma?' he demanded, his face black with anger. She nodded. She couldn't stay because of Gemma. 'It. My God! You self-centred, idle…' His eyes closed in pain. 'If I hadn't come back early, you would have left her,' he said menacingly. 'Yelling and alone—'

She flinched at the accusation. 'No! I was waiting for

you to come back! She…she was crying! She kept crying!
On and on…'

'But you wouldn't pick her up.'

At her wits' end, her mind confused, Ellen turned her
back on him, unable to meet the bitterness and loathing
in his eyes. Summoning up all her strength, she bent to
pick up her case. Behind her, she heard a sharp intake of
breath and she straightened, terrified of what he might do.

'My God! You…you mean it, then!' he breathed in
horror.

'Yes,' she replied listlessly. 'I'm going to my parents.'

Luc placed Gemma on the play mat and in two ground-
swallowing strides was standing in front of her, fury in
every line of his body. *'Why?'* he raged. 'OK, leave me,
fall out of love with me, be bored by me. I can understand
that—but how can you leave your own baby?'

Numb with misery, she stared back, watching him push
back his hair in a tell-tale gesture that echoed the bewilderment in his face.

'Say something!' he snapped.

'Nothing to say,' she mumbled painfully.

'You can't go! She needs you!' he cried passionately.
'You're fit and well. She's not thriving. Don't you care?
Doesn't your heart *bleed* when she cries? Don't you feel
pity?' He stared at her uncomprehendingly, his frustration
mounting. 'What kind of a monster are you,' he demanded, 'that you rarely pick your own baby up and
barely look at her? Why don't you cuddle her? God,
Ellen, can't you find it in your heart to *love* her?'

She couldn't answer. She didn't know. Only that she
was scared of killing Gemma. Scared of the madness and
violence which kept sneaking up and possessing her without warning. So she'd blocked her daughter from her
mind as far as possible and turned her emotions to ice.

The suffocating sensation was taking over her body
again. Knowing how close she was to screaming, she remained mute and kept her own counsel, willing her legs

not to shake and betray the weakness which clamoured relentlessly within her, and which urged her to stay in the hope she might get better.

So she chanted to herself. I must go. For Gemma's safety. I must go...

Seeing only her mask of cool indifference, he grabbed her roughly then, his eyes brilliant with passion and pain. For a moment they struggled as she tried to escape. But he was very strong and she had no energy to continue.

'The trouble is, you're used to being Daddy's little darling!' He let her go in disgust and she stood as motionless as a statue, fighting her illness with a single-minded desperation. 'Adversity's not your scene. You want to be featherbedded. You're used to having money and we have none. You can't hack it. I suppose you regret leaving your father's expensive home. Romance in a hovel isn't all you imagined, is it?'

'Luc, please...!' she croaked.

'You want life on a platter. And all I've offered you is love and poverty!' he thundered on, almost incoherent now. 'Not enough, is it? Having a baby has made things worse. It forces you to think of someone other than yourself for a change! Too hard for you, is it?' he taunted.

She nodded because she could do nothing else. Fear for her baby—and for herself—had driven her to this. She was going mad. Terror claimed her. She didn't want to be sectioned and psychoanalysed in some awful institution.

Only her father could help now. Pride would stop him from revealing her madness. He'd find a private doctor to help and, she acknowledged bitterly, he'd probably welcome her vulnerability. And she'd see her mother again, be held in her arms...

Luc had gone white around the mouth and was trembling with emotion and exhaustion. Her heart went out to him. She knew he must be unbelievably tired after his

twelve-hour shifts, especially when he always came home
to chaos and then had to start cooking his own supper.

She ached to see him so hurt. Part of her wanted him
to suspect that something was wrong, to take her in his
arms and promise that together they could solve any problem. But when she reached out a tentative hand he drew
back from her as if she were offering poison.

'I don't want to shake hands with you. I don't want to
touch you. Just get out of my sight!' he muttered vi-
ciously. 'Go back to your father. Help him count his
money and live out his lonely, egocentric life! You don't
belong to my world and never have. You're superficial
and selfish and only out for a good time. I might come
from a slum, but at least my family taught me decent
values and I know how to love someone other than myself—'

'Luc—' she began jerkily, her eyes soft with unshed
tears.

'No!' he yelled, clearly close to breaking point. 'Don't
prolong this; I couldn't bear it. There's no point in hanging around! Just go! Get out of my house! I don't want
to see you ever again!'

His brutal words beat into her brain like iron hammers.
The injustice bit deep into her heart. If he'd truly loved
her, he would have tried to stop her. But he didn't. He
couldn't wait for her to leave.

Cold to the bone, she took a last look at her baby. Poor
little mite. She lay on the padded play mat and started to
scream. *Goodbye, Gemma. Forgive me,* she prayed for-
lornly. For a split second Gemma stopped crying. The
coincidence was too much for Ellen to bear. Almost sick
with despair, she turned on her heel and stumbled out, a
well of acrid tears streaming from her eyes and almost
blinding her.

She heard her luggage being flung out on the ground
beside her, because she'd forgotten it in her panic. The

door was slammed shut with a vehemence that rattled its glass panes.

Indifferent to their neighbours' twitching curtains, she remained for a long time outside their tiny terrace house—their love-nest which they'd painted and decorated and loved and laughed in. Inside, Luc could be heard trying to calm Gemma. When the child's screaming stopped, Ellen numbly picked up her case and walked away.

Back to her parents. Back to 'I told you so'.

Her father's self-congratulatory attitude made her feel worse. He'd been proved right—and therefore he assumed the right to dictate her every move. Crushed and defenceless, her mind a fuddled blur, she let herself be pushed around because she didn't care what happened to her any more. She had lost the two people she loved.

But it was almost the last straw when her hair fell out. Great handfuls of it remained on the pillow each morning. Every sweep of her hairbrush drew out clumps of hair, roots and all, leaving disgusting bare patches on her head. That nearly tipped her over the edge, and she wept and wept for her lost love, her child and her femininity.

At that moment, with her breakdown worsening with every day, Luc took a devastating revenge which almost destroyed her reason entirely. He took Gemma away to Italy. Ellen had never believed she could suffer so much and not die of despair.

But she had survived. And she was looking at an altogether different person now. Critically she scrutinised her elfin hairstyle, her perfect skin—thanks to a healthy eating regime—and her up-to-date clothes.

Luc would be the one at a disadvantage, not her. She stood there for a moment, breathing steadily, gathering up her courage. And now she was ready.

Stuffing the chocolate bar and magazine in her big canvas shoulder bag, she malevolently eyed the door, which lurked with intent, like an implacable enemy.

'I hereby name you Luc!' she muttered with loathing.

Then she whipped out her mascara and lipstick for a quick coat all round, and slipped her small feet into a pair of high-heeled shoes before going forth to limbo around the door and meet its namesake head on.

By the time Ellen arrived at the café, Luc was already there. His face was hidden behind an Italian newspaper, but Ellen knew it was a million to one chance that anyone else would be reading *La Stampa* and wearing knife-creased beige trousers with matching socks and designer shoes in this particular part of London!

'Hi, Ell. Usual?' called out the young waitress cheerfully, flicking back her marmalade ponytail.

'Thanks, Tracy.' Feeling unbelievably nervous, she shut the door with exaggerated care. A coffee and doughnut would give her something to hold, to fiddle with. Props could prove useful, she thought.

Luc was knocked sideways by Ellen's appearance. He watched her sashay in and felt that old, familiar grabbing at his guts as the full impact of her amazing sex appeal rocketed around the small café.

It occurred to him that this could be the last time he ever saw her, and he decided to make the most of the opportunity to feast his eyes.

To this end, he studied her avidly. Her hair was incredible, hugging her head in close, feathery blonde wisps which accentuated the clean lines of her beautiful face and neck.

It suited her. The new Ellen excited him. Everything about her gave off a challenge: the carriage of her body, her clothes and that assured manner which suggested she didn't give a damn about anybody's opinion.

Yet she was sending out sexual signals too, in every movement she made, in each glance from those smoky eyes and with every word that came from her pillowy lips. She looked, in fact, as if she'd just climbed out of a tumbled bed.

As well she might.

His teeth ground together and he fought down the rush of jealousy which had come from nowhere to scour his stomach. Her appearance confirmed the spur-of-the-moment decision he'd come to during their telephone conversation.

She wasn't the kind of person he wanted Gemma to be with, not ever again. Ellen's part in the visit was off. He'd have to make other arrangements. Nothing could be more inconvenient! Still, there was one consolation. At least in future he wouldn't have to cope with Gemma's hysterics every time she returned from seeing her flighty, selfish mother.

Slowly his resentful gaze wandered over Ellen's tight, firm rear, and he felt his blood pressure rising as he imagined other men touching her, hearing her moans and whimpers.... Luc clenched his fists, but in his mind he was tasting the softness of her flesh, its satin smoothness eagerly accepting his tongue, his lips...

Shaking, he lifted the newspaper higher and hid behind it, appalled by the strength of his desire. He tried to read but her image danced before his eyes and the latest political scandal didn't have a chance. Wherever he focused, there was Ellen: slender and beautiful and wearing that outrageous lime top and body-moulding skirt, both of which left little to the imagination as far as her shapely curves were concerned.

She was announcing her availability. And he was salivating and lusting after her like any normal male. But the difference was that he knew that she was a piranha and he had no intention of being eaten alive. On the contrary, he meant to eat her.

Ellen had heard the rustle of the newspaper and presumed he was looking in her direction. Contrarily, she ignored him and made her way to the counter instead of going over and saying hello. Behind her back she could feel the atmosphere thickening. The hairs on the nape of her neck came to attention.

She didn't want to turn around. Her first-night nerves seemed to have returned with a vengeance. She felt, she thought, groping for humour to ease her jitters, as if she were about to recite her thirty-four times table before a bunch of university dons.

'How's your love life? Still fighting them off?' asked Tracy enviously, in a voice which could have reached across a windswept airfield.

Ellen gave a silent groan. More grist to Luc's mill! Not that it mattered any more. 'In droves,' she said with a sigh.

Tracy leaned close and produced her version of a whisper. 'That's one of yours, over there. Been asking after you. Eyelashes and foreign accent to die for! Go on, grab him before someone else does—'

'No, thanks. I'm trying to give him up. He's my estranged husband, Tracy,' she said drily. And she winked and made a face to show that she wasn't offended by Tracy's remarks.

'No sweat!' Tracy eyed Ellen in awe. 'You sure can reel 'em in! So who left who?'

Casting a covert glance at the mirror behind Tracy's head, she saw that Luc was watching her, his dark eyes glittering cynically.

'I left him.'

'I knew it! You're mad!' Tracy said with a grin.

Ellen gave a wry smile. 'Many a true word said in jest,' she replied.

With her heart beating in a peculiar rhythm, she picked up her coffee and doughnut and swivelled around carefully, remaining perfectly balanced on her stilettos. A movement told her that, always the gentleman, he'd risen from his seat and was waiting for her to go over. Deliberately avoiding his gaze, she walked towards him

with measured stride, her eyes firmly fixed on the mug
and plate in her hands.

Everything seemed magnified. Her breathing. The supple movement of her body, the unstoppable sway of her
hips. And suddenly she became intensely conscious of the
tightness of her skirt and the brightness of the top she
was wearing.

She argued that her clothes were no different from
those of the younger women at work. The same as
Tracy's even. It annoyed her that she suddenly felt uncomfortable with what she was wearing, when even blue-
blooded babes in the society columns were sporting
equally trendy and far racier outfits. There was nothing
wrong with her gear. She looked great. To hell with it.

'Evening.'

The manner in which he spoke conveyed total disapproval. By focusing her attention on placing the plate and
mug on the table, then sliding gracefully onto the red
plastic seat, she successfully dispelled her knee-jerk dismay at Luc's intense assessment. He could think what he
liked. She didn't need his approbation.

Slowly she elevated her chin, meeting his gaze with a
steely and haughty stare. He returned it with the force of
a flashing laser beam. A shock of recognition ran through
her body, throwing her emotions into a spin. He still hated
her! Hastily she dipped her startled eyes to her doughnut.

'Been waiting long?' she asked, as if she didn't care if
he had.

Thank you, she said to the doughnut silently. Thanks
for being there! She raised it to her lips and took a small,
almost fussy little bite. And, without thinking, delicately
licked the sugar grains from the corners of her mouth with
her small questing tongue.

He didn't reply, but she was aware of some kind of
struggle going on inside him. That surprised her. Without
knowing how or why, she was reading his body, the im-

perceptible movements of his chest and shoulders, the change in his breathing. But then she knew it so well.

The doughnut proved useful again, allowing her to sink her teeth into it and drive away all memories of Luc's beautiful physique. The mystery of his strained silence remained. Inwardly shaken by the impact of his venom, she looked up again and raised one beautifully arched eyebrow to its full extent.

'Something wrong?' she asked coolly.

He looked expensive. Suit, shirt, watch, manicure, groomed hair, the lot. He'd made a good deal of money if his appearance was anything to go by.

She watched the shapely shoulder lift a fraction in an imperceptible shrug. He treated her to a full head-to-middle appraisal, only the table between them preventing him from continuing down to her thighs, bare legs and shoes.

Ellen tensed, finding the thought of a whole-body search by his roving eyes horribly disconcerting. And very, very exciting.

Unnerved by this, she lowered her lashes again, certain that he could identify her disgusting reaction. Too many early nights, she thought gloomily. Along came a half-decent-looking man and all her needs had to kick common sense into touch!

'I wasn't expecting you to be so...' Another long, slow glance. He made a sound in his throat like a husky growl. 'So up-front,' he finished grimly. 'I hardly recognised you.'

That could be a compliment or an insult. She fiddled with her almost non-existent hair from habit, surprised as always not to find a mass of curls beneath her fingers. Disconcerted by the discovery, she struggled not to become a casualty of his wickedly unconscious sensuality.

'I'm not the same person you knew at all.'

'I can see that.'

He had followed the arc of her creamy arm, his hooded

gaze wandering down its curves to her breasts. And he'd smiled to himself, his wonderfully erotic mouth lifting with hunger when his lazy glance somehow tightened her flesh and caused her nipples to peak through the thin fabric. Incensed at being so damn obvious, she folded her arms across her chest, hoping that she looked a million times less flustered than she felt.

'What a change!' he went on slowly, the husky admiration in his voice warming her through and through. She felt pleased. She'd wanted him to be impressed. And then he spoiled it. 'I can see you've become a fully-fledged fun-loving girl,' he drawled, making that sound like a crime.

'Woman!' she corrected, forcing herself to stay remote. You didn't go through hell and out the other side and stay girly.

Luc slowly shook his head. 'I don't think so. Women take life seriously when necessary.'

'You poor old thing! You're so stuffy,' she countered breezily, not bothering to defend herself. Why should she? Let him think she was having a ball. Nothing mattered any more.

'Better stuffy than frivolous,' he replied stiffly.

Watching him, she realised that he wasn't happy; it was written all over his face. He had the gravity of a man who hadn't laughed in ages. She longed to ask him questions, to know what had happened to him. But she bit them back. He'd think her interest was personal, whereas it was... She frowned. What was it?

Old-fashioned nosiness. Yes. That was it.

'I disagree. Life is to be enjoyed and I'm doing just that,' she said, producing a big, beaming smile. And couldn't resist, 'How about you?'

Luc looked puzzled, as if enjoyment wasn't on his agenda and it had never occurred to him that it should be. He ignored her question. 'You still wear your wedding ring.'

Her fingers went to it automatically. It had been the cheapest they could find. But she would never remove it. 'And you wear yours,' she said in surprise.

He shrugged. 'It's a useful deterrent, as I'm sure you've discovered for yourself. I gather you're much sought after. Being free suits you—whereas living with Gemma and me was unpleasantly inhibiting for you—'

'Let's forget that!' she said hastily, with a dismissive wave of her hand. She wasn't going to sit there while he reminisced about bad times. Her knees began to tremble and she squeezed them together. 'Water under the bridge,' she said, more airily than she'd intended. She blushed. It sounded as if their break-up had meant nothing to her.

'More like an ocean,' he muttered.

For a moment she thought she saw regret in his eyes. Hers must have responded and gentled, because she felt her animosity vanishing like melting snow as his dark gaze captured and held hers.

They were very close to one another. Maybe a foot apart. Some Italians, she thought hazily, had no sense of personal space. They were close enough for her to find herself inching forwards to confirm the whisper of his breath across her throbbing mouth. Close enough to smell him. It was something she wasn't prepared for: the familiar scent which was Luc, and Luc alone, clean, fresh and male.

It did terrible things to her. It reached parts she'd thought would never feel anything again. She could touch him if she chose to, perhaps run her finger along his mouth and trace the impossibly sultry outline of his lips. Her own mouth became soft and pouting at the thought.

And then she remembered why they were both here— to sever all links. That was why he looked as though he were pleading with her. To say 'Shame it all happened, let's call it quits, let me make a life of my own with Miss Right and Gemma'.

Ellen flinched. Caught like a helpless animal in the path

of his monstrous aura, she forced herself to lean back in her chair, cutting off the invisible strings which had been drawing them together.

When he continued to study her with narrowed eyes, she floundered around for something to say. All she could come up with was a banality.

'You're better dressed than I remember. Otherwise you've hardly altered at all,' she trotted out brightly, pretending to make an indifferent and cursory examination.

But everything she'd seen had been etched indelibly on her mind, and she wished he'd changed beyond all recognition too. He showed the same striking masculinity which had attracted her instantly. That identical terrifying chemistry which had bonded them together, in an instant, fatal attraction. An unchanging, awesome energy emanating from every pore of his body.

Yet there was something essentially different about his eyes and mouth. Ellen's heart missed a beat. They showed no life. No softness.

'Sometimes I wish I were the same man you married,' he said, almost too quietly for her to hear.

Surprised by a painful echo of that wish, she grabbed the doughnut and bit deeply into it. Jam dripped on her chin and she absently set about it with her finger. She became aware that Luc had become unnaturally still. He wasn't even breathing. And something definitely sexual was curling through her body in response to his raw animal attraction.

It wasn't going to get her anywhere so she might as well ignore it. She'd worked too hard to overcome the past for it to overwhelm her now. Deliberately defying all the rules about provocative behaviour, she took as much time as she wanted in licking her finger clean and then met his black, unreadable eyes as though she were invincible.

'You didn't bring me here to wallow in old memories,' she pointed out, amazed at her ability to cover up her confusion. 'And I'm certainly not here to be sociable. Let's get down to business.'

Her throat felt as if it had been sandpapered as she prepared to cut her daughter out of her life. Needing a caffeine rush, she sipped her hot coffee and flicked a brief glance at Luc. He was watching her as if he wanted to remember every detail of every inch. And yet there was a suppressed anger in his hard eyes and she instinctively drew back, scared of the venomous hatred he bore her.

'Of course.' He was all efficiency suddenly, confirming Ellen's suspicions about his purpose. 'It's about Gemma,' he said briskly.

Her stomach lurched. 'I gathered that.'

She kept her tone dry and even, determined not to beg him to keep things as they were. He tapped his fingers on his folded newspaper impatiently, and it was as clear as day that he wanted to end this uncomfortable meeting. But she'd do that. She'd take charge of the situation and move from being victim to victor. Her heart pounded as she spoke again.

'I know what you're going to say. That's why I agreed to meet you,' she said quickly, anxious to get her ordeal over with. 'I think...' She dived in before she played chicken. 'I've decided that it would be better for us all if Gemma never came to see me again.'

There. The deed was done. She sat frozen with horror at the terrible ease with which she'd eliminated the only person she loved in the whole wide world.

Luc, for his part, looked totally dumbfounded. He stared at her for a while then gave a short, mirthless laugh. 'Well, you've taken the wind out of my sails! I was expecting a battle. You're right, of course.' He studied her pale, wan face curiously. 'I suppose I have to thank you for making things less awkward for me.'

'I'm doing this for Gemma,' she said like an automaton.

She felt sick, the nausea clawing its way up to her

throat. Desperate to be alone, to crawl into a corner somewhere and curl up in a miserable ball, she pretended to stare out of the window instead, forcing back the bile and willing him to take the hint from her stiff, cold body. She longed for him to leave so that she could let out her inner scream at last.

All she could see was her reflection and his. The two of them sat in seeming intimacy, huddled over the small table. Her own chalky face looked back at her with two large dark pools where her eyes should be. He was in profile, the lines of his face hard, intimidating and rigid.

'Of course you're thinking of her welfare,' he said with heavy sarcasm, and she bridled because he plainly didn't believe that. His next words proved her to be right. 'But I imagine,' he added silkily, 'it also makes your life easier if you don't have to give up your holidays and leisure time to look after her.'

Holidays? Leisure time? Chance would be a fine thing. Bleakly she wondered what it would be like to be totally alone. No Gemma. Not ever again. The pains were slicing into her heart and she had to put her hand there, on the pretext of sliding her fingers up to rub her collarbone.

'I don't want to do this. But Gemma's obviously disturbed by being uprooted from all she knows. She hates being left in a foreign country,' she began miserably.

'You're her mother. She'd accept the situation if you loved her, if you welcomed her with warmth and affection. Donatello says you're cool and indifferent—'

'No! I'm...' Defeated by the thought of the lengthy explanation, she let her voice trail away.

How could she explain her caution? Whenever she'd put her arms out and offered a warm, loving smile, Gemma had stared at her stonily and clutched at Donatello's legs. From way back in the early days Gemma had begun yelling even as he'd handed her over, and it had even crossed Ellen's mind that Donatello must have pinched the child for such a sudden and alarming response to occur. But gradually she'd realised that Gemma hated the visits. And Ellen had tried hard not to demand too much from her child, hoping that in time they could come to an understanding.

Now they'd be strangers for ever. She coughed to disguise a sob, and sipped coffee to moisten her raw throat. And suddenly she knew she couldn't bear to talk about this any longer. She wanted him to leave.

'It's what you wanted, isn't it?' she said, her voice near to breaking up. She needed privacy. Time to recover, to blank out her mind and get used to what she'd done. 'There's nothing else to say. Why don't you go?' she suggested sharply.

'Oh, I will, and gladly,' he growled. Then he leaned nearer, invading her space with his tantalising male scent and the hateful soft murmur of his mocking voice. 'Know something amusing, Ellen? I thought I was going to hurt you by telling you this evening that I intended to end your access rights.'

Her chest compressed. She'd been right. And she'd foiled his nasty little plan.

'I'm sure you were looking forward to that enormously. I'm so sorry to have spoiled your fun by jumping the gun.'

She turned to give him one of her cold stares, but she felt far from cool inside. He'd looked forward to inflicting pain on her, she thought bitterly. So she was damned if she'd give him the satisfaction of knowing her heart was being chewed to shreds.

'My mistake,' he drawled. 'I should have known you wouldn't care. You've never cared, have you, Ellen? You always resented carrying out your motherly duties.'

'That's not true!' she whispered.

'The facts speak for themselves.' His eyes glittered and he added, 'It's ironic that when I rang you earlier, it was at Gemma's own request.'

Ellen's spine stiffened. *'Gemma?'* she repeated in amazement. 'About what?'

The metallic glint in his eyes frightened her. She saw his intention to turn the knife and she braced herself for what he was about to say or do.

Luc smiled faintly, but it was a dark and bitter smile which sent shivers up her back. 'She wanted to stay with you.'

Ellen's mouth opened and closed in amazement. Then she cottoned on to his game. 'You're lying,' she said coldly. 'That's impossible! Last time—'

He cut her off with a gesture of his hand, pushed back his chair and stood up abruptly, as if he didn't want to remember that occasion. 'I know what happened. You upset her. I never did find out the cause.' His face twisted.

'Then it doesn't make sense—'

'I know that!' he said testily. 'I am as puzzled as you. But she did beg to be with you.'

'Beg?'

'Believe it or not, I don't intend trying to convince you, since you don't want her—'

She didn't hear the rest. The breath had deserted her lungs, leaving her gasping for oxygen. With grey eyes growing wider and wider, she stared uncomprehendingly at Luc, her lips parting in bewilderment as she struggled for understanding, for air, for speech.

'You're not…kidding?' she burst out breathlessly, her eyes starry with hope. 'She…she wanted to stay with me?'

She felt her blood rushing through her like hot oil, pushing up her pulse-rate. A hard, choking lump came to her throat and she swallowed convulsively.

The dark eyes were full of scorn. 'Forget it,' he said in dismissal. 'You've made your decision to write her off. I can't say I'm not sorry. I don't think your life-style adapts very well to part-time motherhood, do you? I'd hate Gemma to interfere with your social activities,' he finished with a scathing glance, obviously intending to leave.

Frantically Ellen jumped up and planted herself in front of him. 'Wait a minute!' she cried jerkily.

It was unbelievable. A turning point. After all that had happened, *Gemma wanted her*!

Somehow she sucked in air, frantically trampling on her joy. He mustn't know what this meant to her. If he did, he'd pull the plug. He'd like nothing better.

'I can't waste any more time.' A small frown pulled his dark brows together. 'I must make other arrangements for her urgently—'

'No.' Her hand detained him. He looked at it pointedly and she let it drop in embarrassment. But she had to put her pride, if not her emotions, on the line. This could be a breakthrough in her relationship with Gemma. 'Please sit down,' she said in breathless excitement. 'I have to explain!'

With a show of irritation, Luc looked at his watch. 'Make it short,' he said grumpily, and perched on the edge of his chair with a show of reluctance.

Ellen gathered her scattered thoughts, knowing how important the next few minutes would be. She'd have an uphill task in persuading Luc that she was reliable enough to look after Gemma. But everything depended on her doing so. Taking a huge breath, she began.

'First, Cyril—the man you spoke to on the phone—is my landlord, not my lover. I live in a block of flats,' she said as calmly as she could. 'That's why he answers the phone. It's a communal one.'

'Really.' Luc eyed her steadily, without emotion. 'If this is true, why didn't you tell me at the time?'

Ellen bit her lip. Good question. 'You were the one who jumped to conclusions and flung accusations at me,' she reminded him. 'I had no reason to explain anything. You annoyed me. If you want to know, I didn't bother to disillusion you because I didn't care what you thought.

And because, to be honest, I took a perverse pleasure in knowing you hated the thought of me having fun,' she finished ashamedly.

'Petty.'

'Yes. It was,' she admitted, willing to eat humble pie if that helped.

'And this...landlord's...heavy breathing?' Luc drawled.

'He's unfit,' she explained, trying to keep the panic out of her voice. He wasn't buying it. And she had to convince him! 'He wheezes because activity makes him short of breath.'

'Yeah.'

She bit her lip, remembering Cyril's remark. 'When you heard him complaining about the calls I get from men—'

'Oh, yes. Double-glazing salesmen, are they?' he suggested, looking down his nose at her.

'No,' she answered, stifling her impatience. 'People— OK, men—I meet at work, parties—friends of friends at the local pub, that kind of thing—'

'You don't have to detail your busy love life for me,' Luc said coldly.

'I wish I didn't,' she cried in frustration, 'but it seems you've formed the impression that I'm promiscuous—or at the least that I have a string of boyfriends. I want you to know that I'm not and I don't. I meet them, they call, I turn them down.'

He looked sceptical. 'And the snow is freezing in hell.'

'It's true!' she cried, getting desperate. He might as well know the whole story. Bang went her pride, then. 'I've been ill for a long time, Luc, and I haven't been fit enough to make any relationships with men, even if I'd wanted to! I lead a very boring and proper life. I'm only just getting on my feet and carving a future for myself—'

'So that's why Gemma is becoming a hindrance,' he commented.

'No,' she answered gently. Without her knowing it, her face and voice, her whole demeanour, softened with tenderness. 'She'd never be that.'

'You have changed your attitude rather suddenly, haven't you?'

Abandoning caution, she leaned forwards eagerly. This was an opportunity she mustn't miss. Gemma had asked for her. She could risk showing Gemma how much she was loved. Fixing him with her wide, dove-gentle gaze, she leaned across the table, gazing at him pleadingly.

'Please, Luc, try to understand. I decided to stop seeing her because I thought she hated it here and I wanted to spare her distress. This seemed the time to do it. But I swear I did nothing to upset her last time. In fact, she was in a state when she arrived. Now the situation has changed. She's asked to be with me and I'm happy to have her if that's what she wants,' she finished confidently.

There was a strange light in his dark eyes. For a long while he contemplated her, as if trying to come to a decision, a frown creasing his forehead, his lips parted over perfect pearly teeth. Ellen's eyes were glued to his as she waited breathlessly for his judgement, afraid that she'd handed him a powerful weapon by revealing that she would like to see her daughter. Had she gone too far—or not far enough?

'I don't know,' he said slowly.

She bit back her annoyance, acknowledging that perhaps she'd be doubtful if she were in his position. 'Try me,' she urged, trying to sound as normal as possible. Her eyes sparkled, brilliant with optimism. He liked to please his daughter. He couldn't refuse, could he? 'You can ring Gemma every hour, if you like, to check that she's all right,' she said recklessly, 'and to make sure I'm not knocking back double whiskies in an opium den.' Encouraged by the small quirk of his mouth, she said persuasively, 'She'll have a great time, I promise. Give me this chance.'

To her surprise, he reached out and tentatively touched her face. 'We were spectacularly wrong for each other, weren't we?' he mused, almost as if he wanted to convince himself of that fact. Ellen swallowed, feeling suddenly light-headed, as if she had indeed been knocking back neat whiskies. 'I suppose we were too young when we ran away to get married,' he continued, holding her startled gaze with his. 'We thought we could conquer the world. And it conquered us.'

He was right. 'The arrogance of youth,' she said, a little tremulously. 'We were nuts to imagine that the rich, indulged daughter of a wealthy man could slip easily into life with—'

'A lorry driver without a penny to his name.'

'Yes,' she said with a forced laugh. 'Madness!'

'Sex,' he murmured, 'makes sane people behave recklessly.'

It was making her feel dizzy and ready to do something rash right now—like place her hands either side of his smooth jaw and kiss that wildly desirable mouth. She felt appalled. Whatever had happened to drive them apart, there was still a fatal chemistry pulling them back together, even now with all the heartache they'd caused one another.

Ellen resisted it with all her might, but she wanted his touch. Wanted that soft, warm and alarmingly near mouth to cover hers...

'Luc—'

He started at her involuntary hoarse whisper and sat back sharply in his seat, as if she presented a danger to his sanity.

'We destroyed each other,' he said harshly, his eyes black slits between the long, fringing lashes. 'We have to admit that our needs and values were vastly different. We made the mistake of thinking that being good in bed together equated with love. It was nothing but lust. The biological urge can be very powerful.'

Ellen felt as if he'd hit her. They had been in love. Hadn't they? She had. Surely he... Suddenly she registered that he was waiting for a comment from her. Opting for self-preservation, she gave a brilliantly casual laugh.

'True!' she acknowledged, a small part of her heart dying with the admission. 'It's an all-too-common mistake.'

There was a small shrug of his elegant shoulders. 'Not to be repeated.'

It was a clear message. Yes, they still aroused one another, but he was damned if he'd let his desires drive his mind. She glanced up, but he was refolding his newspaper slowly and deliberately and she couldn't see the expression in his eyes.

'Gemma. What about Gemma?' she asked as casually as she could. 'Shall we give it a go?'

He stared at the tablecloth, absently tracing the flower pattern with his long forefinger. 'I'm not sure. She's very sensitive at the moment—'

'I'll be careful. Luc, please, if she wants this...!' she cried, terrified he'd dash her hopes. He looked up, and seemed shocked by the passion in her face. Blinking back an upswell of tears, she managed to give him a lop-sided smile. 'If we can do nothing else, we can make her happy, can't we?'

'I would want to check up on you,' he said slowly, almost slurring his speech. But Ellen was too much on tenterhooks to wonder why. He scowled and she held her breath, but he said, 'If you should let me down—'

'I won't!' she cried, beaming with delight at the grudging capitulation in his tone.

His scowl deepened. 'I'm taking a big chance here. She's the most precious person in my entire life and I'd protect her to the death. Hurt her in any way,' he warned softly, 'and I'll make you suffer so much that you'll wish you'd never set eyes on either of us. *Capis'?*'

Chills flashed down her spine. He meant every word of that threat. Her huge eyes flinched at his piercing stare and she let her terrified gaze drift down in alarm. Unfortunately, she found herself focusing on his broken nose, which reminded her forcibly of his rough childhood, the background which had forged him into the man he now was. Fights and vendettas had filled his childhood in Naples. Revenge was in his soul.

But suddenly she allowed herself a little wry smile. He'd never need to carry out his threat. She was home and dry. Her whole body straightened and she began to breathe more easily.

'Understood,' she said, feeling triumphant. 'When will this be?'

A wild joy started to creep through her. She wanted to dance because she hadn't lost her final chance at motherhood after all. Overwhelmed with an urge to sing, to yell aloud, do somersaults all around the café, nevertheless she remained demurely on her chair. She couldn't believe it! Her daughter had *asked* for her! Miracle of miracles!

'Tonight,' Luc said, delivering his bombshell.

Ellen's mouth gaped open. 'But…you know I'm working!' she cried in dismay. It was too short notice! How dared he walk in and expect her to drop everything—?

'You said.' He was cool and businesslike again. 'I have a breakfast meeting early in the morning. It must be tonight. What time do you finish?'

'Ten!' Too late, she thought, and wanted to wail. Gemma would be asleep by then. She'd lose her chance…

Luc grunted. 'I'll tell her what's happening when I return to the hotel and she'll go to sleep quite happily, I'm sure. I'll wrap her up and bring her to you. All you'll need to do is to put her to bed—she'll be in her nightdress already.' He angled his head speculatively. 'This is a rather short working session, isn't it? Whatever—?'

'Luc, I have to go,' she said, interrupting before he could ask what she could be doing in such a brief time. The main thing was to keep him from discovering where and how she lived. Delighted that she'd coaxed him round, she said decisively, 'Look, bring her here, to the café. I'll order a taxi home.'

His eyes narrowed. 'That's ridiculous. I can drive you.'

'No.' She set her mouth in a stubborn line.

'Something there I shouldn't know about?'

'My sense of independence,' she retorted, meeting his suspicious stare boldly. 'Don't try to take that away from me, Luc.'

He looked at her doubtfully and she felt afraid again. She couldn't stop trembling. If she had any sense at all she should tell him he was asking the impossible. Changing her shifts at the supermarket would be a nightmare, and she risked losing her job. But how could she turn down the opportunity to make friends with her daughter? Quivering with nerves, she decided to leave him no option.

'Gemma's used to the arrangement. We do it every time. Help! I'm late,' she said, needing to jump up and release some tension. 'I don't want to overrun. Look at it like this: you want a favour from me. You want me to take time off work at a moment's notice and I will, but we do this my way. I'll see you here at ten. All details then, yes?'

Anxious to escape, she scrambled out of the chair with a clatter and he made no attempt to stop her. She'd done it!

Luc's eyes followed her all the way. She knew that because she hardly knew how to walk. Her legs seemed to be made of wool. But her head was definitely floating above Cloud Nine!

It would be make or break time. This time she'd pull

out all the stops and show Gemma that she loved her—
even if it meant risking another rejection, breaking her
heart. Perhaps she could explain simply that she'd left
because she'd been ill... She sighed, chewing at her lower
lip. It wouldn't be easy. But something would come to
her.

'Bye, Ell!' called Tracy.

'Bye!' Ellen grinned at the girl's theatrical wink and
swept out, tingling all over.

She stepped off the pavement in a dream. Unfortunately the traffic didn't take any notice of her rosy aura,
and drivers swerved, cussed and hooted at her as she
crossed the road. Brought down to earth, she scuttled to
the safety of the opposite side, throwing apologetic looks
in all directions.

She couldn't resist taking a quick glance over at the
café, to see if Luc had watched her stupid jaywalk. And
of course he had. His unmistakable dark figure stood at
the plate glass window in a pose of utter disapproval.

She'd blown it again! He'd think she was stupid and
irresponsible! She contemplated giving him a little wave,
but thought that would make her seem even more frivolous. Her only hope was that he'd be too anxious to please
Gemma to cancel the arrangement out of pique.

He wouldn't do that to her, she told herself. He
couldn't be that cruel. And she danced happily up
the steps of the community centre, certain that she
and Gemma were about to begin a wonderful new relationship.

CHAPTER THREE

IT HAD taken all of Luc's will-power not to hurry after Ellen and persuade her to play hookey from work that night. From the moment she'd turned her seductive, smoky eyes on him he'd wanted her with a suffocating and overwhelming passion. In an alarmingly short time this had grown almost into an obsession, while he sat there like a stuffed dummy and pretended to be as indifferent as a eunuch.

He allowed himself a small, self-deprecating grimace. She'd captured him, just as she had that first time he'd seen her in that sassy little skirt on the road to Windsor.

Amazingly, she was her old self again: assured, strong-willed and incredibly beautiful. All the time he'd found it hard to keep his mind on what they were discussing. He'd had an irresistible urge to leap over the table at her and pin her to the floor.

A small voice inside him said that she'd wanted him too, and what would it matter if they both indulged their physical needs and had a one-night stand? He glared at the busy street, empty of life and colour now she'd gone.

It was inconceivable that she hadn't had lovers. Yet she'd been so insistent on that fact that he'd believed her against all the odds. Whatever the truth, he felt sure she'd behave herself for the duration of Gemma's short visit. His threat had scared her and so it should. One foot out of line and he'd give her hell.

'More coffee?' called the girl behind the counter.

'No thanks.' Turning with a polite smile of farewell, he picked up his paper and then hurried back to his hotel to give Gemma the good news.

*   *   *

59

Once inside the community centre, Ellen allowed herself to give way to her feelings. Laughing and running in an uncontrollable surge of sheer happiness, she felt suddenly fired up with optimism. Gemma wanted her! The most wonderful words she'd heard since Luc had asked her to marry him.

A tinge of wistfulness shadowed her eyes and then she shook it off. OK, she couldn't have everything. The old Luc had gone for ever and she'd never get him back. But this little piece of good fortune must be cherished and nurtured.

She and Gemma had a future after all!

Greeting everyone joyfully, she apologised for her lateness and scurried to the back room to change, emerging in her briefs and with a towelling gown around her. Behind the discreet screen, she arranged herself on the satin-covered dais and draped a length of satin over her body.

'OK, Paul, ready,' she called.

She lay with her eyes closed, posing in a blissful dream, oblivious of everyone and everything as she planned what she and Gemma would do, who she could call on to do her shifts, how she could make her week's money stretch to feed two.

After her ten-minute break, spent admiring photos of one woman's new grandson and happily joining in the chatter about babies, she resumed her pose.

Some people, she mused, seeing her now, would presume her to be wanton. But it was years since she'd felt sexy or wanton. Immediately Luc came to mind and she remembered vividly. Total surrender. Fusion of bodies. A wild celebration of the difference between man and woman. Tenderness in the aftermath, sweet kisses, sweet nothings, the glorious, unmistakable taste and smell of a man...

Her mouth became full and hungry, as if she'd recently been pleasured. Her whole body took on the glow of a woman in love as her muscles remembered and relaxed. The throb of her pulses sounded in her brain, the rhythm at once primitive and insistent.

Her heavy black lashes fluttered lazily. She turned her head slightly to one side, looking into the room but seeing nothing, her mind absorbed with the rare sense of passion coursing through her.

Outside, Luc tapped impatient fingers. She was late. And he waited for no one.

'Momento,' he threw back to Donatello, waiting in the back of the car with the sleeping Gemma. 'Torno fra dieci minuti.'

The building was emptying. 'I'm looking for Ellen Maccari. Can you help me?' he said to the woman at the enquiries desk.

She looked at him oddly. 'Room 2.' She pointed. 'They're overrunning. You can't go in—'

But he was in a hurry. Ignoring the 'No Entry' sign on the door because he refused to wait any longer, he pushed it open. The door swished silently back and he found himself struck dumb with astonishment at the scene which met his eyes.

A near-naked woman sprawled alluringly on a sheen of black satin, its gleaming darkness contrasting strikingly with her ivory skin.

Ellen.

He inhaled in silent wonder. She slept. But wicked thoughts were filling her dreams because her mouth had become plushly soft and an air of languid pleasure surrounded her. He felt his heart beat rapidly as his hot gaze absorbed and coveted everything he saw.

This was what he'd dreamed of, night after night. This was the image which had woken him, sweating and swearing, because he hated himself for wanting something so worthless. This was what he still wanted. Perhaps he was a masochist, he thought darkly.

Or he'd gone so long without sex that his body was beginning to rebel. Yes. That was it.

Scheming little minx! Surely she'd done this deliberately! He examined this line of thought. Everything added up: arranging for him to hand over Gemma in the café, being late, letting him see her like this... But why? To make him jealous? To point out what he was missing? Or...to entrap him, perhaps, as Donatello had warned?

He gazed at her, emotions tumbling over themselves. Hatred, anger and desire. She had flung her arms back in abandon, her firm round breasts lifting beneath the satin as if offering themselves to a lover's hands.

Bleakly he imagined feasting on each dusky soft nipple, and his tongue moistened his dry lips as he pictured kissing those sleepy peaks and bringing them back to life till they were hard to his tongue and tantalising the highly sensitive parts of his mouth.

Stifling a groan, he raked the rest of her body with glittering eyes, mentally placing his hands on her small waist, stroking her smooth silken thighs and...

He swallowed, passions smouldering within him. His breath hissed out painfully, and as people in the room turned, startled at the unexpected sound, he suddenly sprang into action.

Ellen woke with a start to find Luc was bearing down on her, his face contorted with rage. Before she could sit up—or even work out where she was and what she was doing—he was upon her, the sound of clattering easels and loud protests echoing in his wake.

Yards of satin were being gathered around her body and wrapping it like a cocoon, and then she was being lifted in Luc's arms while he muttered fiercely at her in Italian—words which were beyond her limited vocabulary.

'Luc! Put me down!' she spluttered, as he bore her

unerringly towards the open door of her small dressing room.

'How could you do this?' he fumed, glaring down at her. 'So this is how you spend your so-called boring evenings! Displaying yourself to—'

'It's an art class!' she protested in astonishment.

'Put her down!' ordered Paul from somewhere behind her.

Breathing hell-fire and brimstone, nevertheless Luc let her slither down his body, still trussed up like an Egyptian mummy. She couldn't speak for a moment because she was reeling from the erotic sensation of his hard warmth against her yielding flesh. And... She quivered, thrown into a trembling confusion. He was intensely aroused, and that fact alone made her feel weak.

Her startled eyes met his. And she saw him fighting his desire, hating himself for wanting her.

'Get dressed!' he snarled.

'Is it time to finish, Paul?' she asked, haughtily ignoring him.

'Ye-es, I suppose it is,' Paul said, clearly nonplussed by Luc's interruption. 'But—'

'But! Butt out!' snapped Luc. 'I'm her husband.'

Paul's eyes widened. 'Ellen,' he said in concern. 'Do you need our help?'

'No, I can deal with this, thanks,' she said, pink with mortification.

The infuriated Luc caught hold of her around the waist and lifted her in the air, carrying her trussed and upright body into the little room, where he kicked the door shut and set her down again. Reaching up to the hook on the wall, he pulled down the hanger holding her top and skirt and held it out for her.

'Dress!'

Her mouth twitched with an irrational urge to laugh. The whole scenario was quite ridiculous! There she was, trussed up in black satin and incapable of moving, and he wanted her to dress! She tried ineffectually to escape from the cloth around her. The satin slipped and slid erotically over her body but somehow neglected to free her arms.

'You're out of the Ark, you know that?' she commented, concentrating on de-mummifying herself. 'There's nothing wrong in what I've been doing, so calm down. It's my job.'

'Letting men draw you, leer at you?' He lifted a scornful eyebrow.

Not to be outdone, she lifted one of her own. 'Men and women. My friends. They're *artists*!' she pronounced, marking him down as a Philistine.

'Artists or not, the men must have found you sexually attractive—'

'As you do?' she murmured sweetly, before she could stop herself. Oh, curse her big mouth, she thought in exasperation.

Luc drew in a harsh breath. Then he turned the key in the door. To Ellen's horror, he flung her clothes to the floor, took a step closer and pulled her against his body, slowly, deliberately releasing her satin wrapping and letting it drop in a sensual caress down her hips and thighs till it rested like a dark liquid at her feet.

'Is this what you've been deliberately provoking me to do?' he muttered.

Her half-naked body was pressed against his. She was incapable even of breathing. Spirals of excitement were rising uncontrollably within her. It was as if she had no control over herself at all. A tremor ran through her, and he gave a shuddering intake of breath in response but kept his eyes fixed resolutely on hers.

'Of...course n-not!' she squeaked in alarm.

'Afraid at what you've unleashed? Or do you have a problem with your throat now?' he mocked.

Her face flamed. He was no gentleman to notice!

'Don't be perverse! Let me dress!' she pleaded, aghast at how pathetic she sounded.

'I marvel at your logic. A few moments ago you were allowing strangers to examine you inch by inch—'

'That's different!' she protested, wriggling. And she stopped, quickly, because he'd groaned involuntarily at her movement.

'Why is it different?' he rasped.

'You—you know why! That was impersonal; this isn't. And...we're...*touching*!'

'You're lucky I'm not beating your backside and shaking the life out of you!' he said grimly. 'I don't know what game you're playing, but it sure as hell has backfired!' he seethed. 'If you thought to entrap me by flaunting yourself—'

'No way!' she cried vigorously. 'I wouldn't lift my little finger to beckon you if you were the—'

'Last man on earth, yes—'

'In the entire Galaxy!' she snapped. 'I'd go on a date with a Martian first!'

'Don't protest too strongly,' he said with contempt. 'It makes me suspicious. Whatever your intentions, you were playing me for a sucker. You had actually convinced me that I'd misjudged you, that you were honest and decent—'

'I am!' she insisted, too numb, too stunned to struggle. Waves and waves of desire were softening her body and enfeebling her. It seemed her brain had turned to mush along with her power to move.

'Yeah. You, me and Delilah. You think I'd trust my daughter to the likes of you?' he said incredulously. 'You must think I'm mad.'

She tried to get her mind in gear. What was he saying? That she and Gemma... She groaned. He couldn't go back on his word.

'You can't disappoint her!' she cried plaintively, crushing from her mind the unbearably delicious sensation of

her near-nudity against the formality of his black pin-
stripe suit.

'Watch me.'

Furiously she pushed him away and snatched up her
clothes, her heart pounding like a steam hammer. 'Turn
your back while I dress!' she ordered, dangerously near
to tears.

In answer, he folded his arms and leaned against the
door, as if waiting for a floorshow to begin, an unnerving
curl to his sexy mouth.

Well, she supposed he'd seen her body plenty of times
before. She pushed back the impression that he seemed
to be debating whether or not to pounce on her. She was
damn well going to fight her corner, floorshow or not!

'Now you listen to me,' she said grimly, turning her
top the right side out. 'There's nothing wrong with mod-
elling!' One arm in. The other. She flung him a defiant
glance and gulped at the hungry glitter in his eyes. Her
hands shook as she eased the top over her head and managed to cover her throbbing breasts at last. 'Haven't you
ever admired a classic statue?' she demanded. 'The Venus
de Milo? Or a painting by Rubens? How do you think
they were produced? With the aid of plastic dummies and
a fertile imagination?'

'My theory is that artists have to desire their models,'
he said softly as she bent to pick up her skirt. 'That's how
they produce such beautiful work. It's all a question of
projecting the passion they feel...'

He stopped, and she looked up to find that he was
looking at the swell of her breasts. There was something
in his eyes which unnerved her and dried her throat.

'No, Luc,' she warned, reading his intention and
straightening in alarm.

But he ignored her, taking one, two steps closer while
she felt the breath exhale from her lungs and through her
parted lips as her muscles seemed to become liquid. They
stood tantalising inches apart. She noticed hazily that they

were leaning towards one another, their breath now mingling in small, hot spurts.

His lips were parted like hers. She felt her head tilting back all on its own, and then she felt all her will-power desert her as he reached out to cradle her face and his mouth came nearer and nearer till it touched hers in a tormenting whisper.

Ellen moaned, wanting more than that. And somehow he knew that because their lips met in a long, slow kiss which fired her nerves and electrified her entire body.

Every bone and sinew she possessed was urging her to respond. With a desperate groan, she reached up her arms and twined them around his neck, forcing him to deepen the kiss. Her body moved demandingly against the soft fine wool of his jacket while his hand came to rest in the small of her back just above the top of her briefs.

Gently, skilfully, he parted her mouth with his tongue. Shocked out of her daze, she tried to stop him, but she didn't get any further than emitting a low moan of pleasure. Her body was conspiring to weaken her resistance.

And then he released her. For a moment they stood staring at one another, her desire turning to horror when she saw the mocking smile which touched his scornful mouth.

'I do hope you're not that enthusiastic with every man you meet,' he remarked in a monotone, his eyes a hard, uncompromising black.

She floundered for an answer. A 'no' would mean that he was special. A 'yes' would mean she was easy. 'Why did you do that?' she asked, her voice trembling with rage at her own stupidity. He'd planted a trap and she'd jumped right into it. Her eyes filled with tears and she clenched her fists. Why did he always choose to hurt her?

'I did it because I wanted to. And because you wanted to as well,' he replied, the angles of his cheekbones stark in the brilliance of the overhead light.

All that was true. But he didn't have to point it out to her! 'Bully!' she muttered.

'Save it,' he drawled. 'You weren't exactly fighting me.'

'I was scared!' she cried, finding a way out at last. 'I go to pieces when someone threatens me physically, you know that!' she shot, gaining momentum. 'I told you long ago how the kids at school made my life hell! You know I can't stand people using their superior strength to dominate someone else! You of all people know how desperate I was at school and why I kept running away. And yet you had to yell and push me around and force yourself on me, knowing I'd be rooted to the spot with fear! I loathe you, Luc. You're a predatory swine!' she stormed.

It was a good line to take, but he knew she'd been luring him on with every sway of her fabulous body and each flutter of those flirty black lashes. Right at this moment he hated her for making him want her, for flaunting herself at him like a good-time girl on the make. Whatever her agenda had been in enticing him into the art class, it had been conceived with malice. And for that she'd pay.

He brooded on her flushed, sensual face. She deserved a suitable revenge. Something to teach her a lesson. A plan formed in his mind.

This time she'd made a mistake in thinking she could run rings around him. He let a small smile of satisfaction curl the corners of his mouth. It would be enjoyable turning the tables on her.

Maybe once he'd laid her ghost to rest and wiped her from his life, he'd be able to get Gemma's emotions back on an even keel. And, once free of Ellen, he might even fall in love with a decent woman.

'You shouldn't play with fire,' he advised laconically. Then he assumed an expression of regret. 'What a pity. You've blown it, Ellen. You're not fit to look after my daughter. I'm taking her back to the hotel.'

'She'll be expecting to see me when she wakes!' she cried in agitation. 'We agreed—!'

'That was before this farce,' he said, with a wave of his hand in the direction of the studio, trying not to register that she was still half dressed.

The white frills of her briefs presented a dainty pattern against her honey-coloured skin. His fingers curled and he folded them into his palms. It was either that or he'd be slipping an exploratory finger between that inviting lacy edge and her firm flesh and sliding down to...

'You've tied my hands,' he went on, wishing that she had done just that and speaking even more harshly than he'd intended. 'But what else can I do?' His concentration was slipping, and no wonder. Fortunately she seemed oblivious to the huskiness in his voice. 'Dammit, Ellen, have you no shame? Put your skirt on!' he said irritably, and she flushed as if she'd forgotten all about it.

He turned abruptly, as though in anger, putting his back to temptation. His ears were straining to hear every sound. The slither of her skirt over her thighs. The snap of a fastener. The fumble of her hands as she smoothed the material flat. He all but groaned.

Appalled, he sought to control himself, stalking over to the window and scowling out at the black night. He'd never known he could feel such devastating sexual jealousy. When he'd realised that other men were ogling her body, he'd wanted to lash out and flatten them all, to yell in frustration and fury that she belonged to him and no one else was ever going to see her like that again.

He passed a hand over his eyes and noticed that it shook. If he didn't do something about this, he'd never get back to normality.

He had to have her. And then he must walk away, as she had walked out on him. OK, he was talking stubborn Neapolitan pride here—but until he felt justice had been done he wouldn't be able to put the past behind him.

Slowly his head lifted and he turned around. She was

crossly slipping her feet into a pair of very feminine sandals, which gave her feet and calves a beautiful curve. He swallowed, remembering how he'd used to coax off her shoes very slowly and take every toe into his mouth, then kiss his way along each sensitive sole to the ankle. Hastily he closed his mind to what had happened next because he needed to stay in control every step of the way.

'You want me to beg, don't you?' she muttered.

He almost betrayed himself then. It was an erotic image: Ellen on her knees before him. Narrowing his eyes he said tersely, 'Try it.'

To his surprise, she did.

'Forget what happened for Gemma's sake,' she said in an appealing little whisper.

'Try harder.'

He saw the flash of anger in her velvety eyes which turned them almost to silver. Her mouth was soft and vulnerable, every inch of her pliant and pleading. Excitement was coursing through him, and it took all his will-power to keep his face impassive.

'You don't want to take her to your breakfast meeting,' she said, her sharp mind assembling an irrefutable argument. 'She wants to be with me. I've done nothing wrong, nothing that would harm her, so stop raising your eyebrows at me and pretending to be insulted by my morals! Just tell me. How long were you planning for this visit?'

He almost told her the truth. But it occurred to him that a surprise departure would be easier to handle. 'A week,' he lied, avoiding her searching eyes.

'Well, I'm prepared to take unpaid leave and to cancel my next session here while Gemma's with me. You won't get a better person to care for her.'

'A trained nanny?' he suggested laconically.

'Too iffy. Gemma wouldn't feel safe and you wouldn't be able to do a check on the nanny in the time.' Sure of herself now, she lifted her chin proudly. 'If you think about it logically, you'll realise I'm your only choice.'

He dragged his eyes reluctantly from the hollow in her throat where a pulse disturbed the silky skin. His mouth remembered the feel of her there, the sweet, heady perfume which was a sensual part of her body and which filled his nostrils every time she damn well moved a muscle.

'Hmm. You're right there,' he conceded with a convincing reluctance. 'And she seemed most anxious to be with you. But I don't see...' And then he pretended to have hit on an idea. 'I have a suggestion. Something which will satisfy my anxieties about your behaviour.'

'I'm not wearing a chastity belt,' she said with wry humour. But the brightness of her eyes indicated that she was eager to go along with anything he said.

And he couldn't help grinning, because the last thing he wanted was for her to be sexually restrained. 'OK, let's go for plan B,' he said in amusement. 'You come to my hotel and stay for the week while you look after Gemma. That will curb any ideas you might have had of entertaining a string of men while Gemma watches TV all day. It's an exclusive hide-away for VIPs and celebrities and the staff are very careful about who comes through the doors.'

'Sounds terrific, but...who's paying?' she asked cautiously.

You are, he wanted to say. But not in the way she might think! 'I'll foot your bills. Whatever you like. How about it, Ellen? I'll be around in the evenings...' His heart skipped a beat as he imagined what he'd be doing then. 'So you'll have time off. Take it or leave it.' And he found himself holding his breath, waiting for her reply.

Her body still hummed from being enclosed by his arms. It felt warm and tingly, as if he'd torched it. She drew in a long breath. Singed, more likely! He'd treated her like a chattel. Her hand twitched with the need to dash it across her mouth. If he ever tried that again, she'd tear his buttons off. Rip out his designer labels...

He shifted impatiently and she pulled herself together. 'I suppose that'll be all right,' she said, managing not to appear thrilled with the success of her rhetoric. And there'd be the bonus of staying in a luxury hotel, all comforts paid for! Under the pretext of collecting her bag, she hid her grin of delight. 'Shall we go, then?'

In the studio everyone had huddled together, chattering excitedly. They stopped and looked up when she and Luc walked out. Ellen's eyes widened at the path of destruction Luc had left in his wake. No one had bothered to tidy up yet—they'd obviously been far too interested in debating the outcome of his dramatic appearance.

'Bye, Paul—everyone,' she called demurely, a twinkle in her eyes.

'You all right?' Paul asked, frowning.

'Never better,' she said truthfully. 'Let me know if there's any damage. Luc will pay. Paul... This is short notice, I know, but I'll have to miss next week. Can you cope?'

'Of course,' Paul assured her warmly. 'We can get someone else. We'd all prefer you, of course...' He caught Luc's icy stare and became flustered. 'It's because you keep very still. You're a professional—'

'The car's outside,' Luc said testily.

Ellen flung a friendly smile at everyone as Luc hurried her out. And there was the Bentley which Donatello always turned up in, with a hired chauffeur in the driving seat. Her heart began to thump hard as Luc captured her elbow and pushed her towards the limousine.

'We'll stop at your flat so you can get your stuff—'

'No,' she broke in, and hastily invented an excuse. 'It's late. I'd feel happier if we went straight to the hotel and settled Gemma.'

'All right by me,' he replied easily. And then he gave one of his slow, sexy smiles and the hand on her elbow tightened a fraction as he said, 'You always slept naked. Nightwear won't be a problem, will it?'

Ellen swallowed and wished she could drag her gaze from his. 'No,' she mumbled, annoyed that she sounded like a frog with asthma.

His smile broadened but it still seemed unduly sensual. 'Good. No need to worry about your wash things, either. They always provide complimentary kits complete with toothbrush in my suite—'

'Hang on.' They stopped on the pavement, level with the bonnet of the car. This was getting worrying. She hadn't expected such intimacy! 'Your suite? How many beds are there? How many rooms?'

'It's the penthouse,' he supplied easily. 'It has one vast sitting room, with a spectacular view over Kensington Gardens and Millionaire's Row, and comes with three bedrooms.'

'You, Gemma and Donatello?' Her mouth tightened at his cheerful nod. 'So where does that put me?' she asked sharply.

'On the floor, the couch, my bed or we move 'Tello out,' he replied in amusement.

'Floor, couch or eject Donatello,' she opted promptly.

He laughed. ''Tello it is. He won't mind. It'll give him a break from having Gemma jumping on his bed in the morning. Well,' he said, with a smug expression, 'we seem to have worked out an arrangement which satisfies us both.' He opened the back door for her and paused. 'We'll have to do something about your clothes, of course.'

'If you take me, you take my clothes,' she said, offended.

His face was wreathed in smiles, and suddenly she realised what she'd said and blushed scarlet. 'I meant, you only have what you stand up in,' he told her softly. 'You can go shopping for what you need in the morning, with my chauffeur to keep you in order. I'll foot those bills too. Gemma loves shopping. She's a true Italian.'

'Why are you being so generous?' It seemed very fishy.

Did he think she'd give him something in return? 'You can't buy me, you know,' she said proudly.

'Why would I want to?' he asked, widening his eyes with suspicious innocence.

She shrugged and shifted her feet in embarrassment. 'You have to admit that it's a bit odd, you forking out your hard-earned cash for someone you don't even like.'

He smiled disarmingly. 'You were always too quick-witted for me to pull the wool over your eyes, weren't you?' The low warmth of his voice slid into her like rich honey. 'I should have known my subtle scheme wouldn't get past you. The truth is, Ellen, that I'd do anything to stop you hiking back to Southwark with Gemma and involving her in your private life.'

'It's not Plague City,' she said in mild protest. But who was she to argue? 'Still, I like the bribe.' Deliberately she upped her enthusiasm, to get him worried about his bank balance. 'A new wardrobe! How lovely!'

'Get in,' he muttered, his steely undertone revealing the contempt he felt for her pretended materialism.

She obeyed, realising she was pushing him a little too far, and eased her slender body into the back. 'Hello, Donatello,' she said in her usual polite way. But her eyes were on the sleeping child beside him. She reached out, hardly hearing the PA's response, and touched Gemma's curls tenderly. 'Hello, sweetheart,' she breathed, melting at the sight of her daughter's slumbering face.

'Seat belt,' ordered Luc from his seat beside the driver.

Her mouth quirked and she smiled at the back of his head. It looked stiff and tense, as if he hated the fact that she'd got her own way and that she'd be looking after Gemma despite his reservations.

He'd like it even less when he saw that his daughter was having a lovely time! Nerves began to chase through her stomach, knotting it up. Gemma *must* have a lovely time! she thought anxiously, twisting her hands together.

Slowly it began to dawn on her how delicately she

must feel her way over the next few days. One step wrong, and Luc would see to it that she'd lose her child for ever.

She shivered. He'd be watching her like a hawk, hoping she'd make a mistake. Dear heaven, he was putting her under the most awful pressure!

CHAPTER FOUR

SHE sat anxiously fiddling with her fingers while Luc began informing Donatello of the arrangement. They spoke in fast, colloquial Italian, and she hardly understood a word. Several times the PA glanced at Ellen doubtfully, as if he wasn't sure she was to be trusted.

She treated him to smiles which she hoped were friendly and confident. Donatello merely flicked his dark gaze back to his employer and listened intently, putting in his own questions here and there.

Luc was lucky to have such a devoted person as his closest aide, she thought. He clearly loved Gemma. Donatello had been absently stroking Gemma's arm all the time he and Luc had been talking. Ellen's heart warmed to the taciturn man, and when Luc appeared to have finished speaking, she turned to the PA with an apologetic smile.

'I'm sorry about your room,' she began.

'No problem.' To her surprise, he gave her a faint smile, whereas before he'd always been coldly hostile. 'It will be for Gemma's benefit,' he said courteously, and she relaxed, chatting to him all the way to the hotel.

It was the most gorgeous place, once a Georgian mansion, she assumed, in an exclusive district of London. The interior had been furnished with eighteenth-century antiques which gave it the atmosphere of an elegant home.

Ellen ogled the exquisite walnut and fruitwood furniture and vast, gilt-framed oil paintings while Donatello retrieved a set of keys from a discreetly positioned desk, where he made arrangements with the liveried porter for his transfer to another room.

'It's lovely,' she said to Luc in awe. 'You must have done well for yourself to be able to afford to stay here.'

He shot her a suspicious look. 'I've worked hard.'

She was a little taken aback by the curtness of his response.

'What do you do?' she asked curiously. 'Gemma said something about you working on a *traghetto*—that's a ferry boat, isn't it?'

'I own a boat.'

'It must bring in a hell of an income!' she said with a smile.

'It must, mustn't it?' Cutting off any further questions, Luc set off with Gemma in his arms towards a set of mahogany doors which turned out to conceal a lift.

Yes, she thought, following him inside. She could believe he'd achieved his ambitions by the sweat of his own brow. It was admirable. To a point.

Before they'd married he'd been a happy-go-lucky kind of man, and they'd had some marvellous fun together. When she'd discovered she was pregnant, three months later, he'd proposed. They'd arranged to elope, and from that moment on he'd begun to work all the hours he could.

At first his dedication had charmed her. He'd been working to provide for them both because she, at seventeen, had no qualifications other than her poise and fancy schooling, neither of which were much good in the cut and thrust of ordinary life. Her job as a temporary sales assistant had brought in only a pittance and she'd known he was worried that she'd find it hard to adapt from a life of comfort and plenty.

But she hadn't cared. All she'd wanted was him.

The trouble was, he'd never seemed to be around. And her pregnancy had prompted him to work all hours to provide for his coming family.

He'd used to come back to their tiny flat looking exhausted and grey. Gone was the man she'd fallen in love with; in his place someone too tired for loving, almost too tired to eat. And the slightest thing had made him irritable. She'd begun to feel frightened that she'd made a huge mistake.

And yet there had been good times. Few and far between, perhaps, but they had been so wonderful that her heart had begun to sing again when they'd come along, and her love for Luc had intensified.

But she'd wondered sometimes, after a long, hard day on her feet, did he love her—or had he been driven to marry her by stubborn pride and a sense of duty because she'd been pregnant?

His mother had totally disapproved. Her parents had both been appalled and had threatened to disown her because Luc was a mere lorry driver. When she'd gone ahead with the marriage, pride had prevented her father from withdrawing his threat.

And, for Ellen, some of her parents' dire warnings had festered in her mind. Had he tired of her, once the novelty of sex had worn off? Did he only lust after her? Had he married her just to ensure a claim to their child? Doubts had come thick and fast. They'd grown out of all proportion during her pregnancy because she'd been so ill.

It couldn't have been much fun coming home to a woman who was always sick and looked like a beached whale, she mused now, following Luc into the penthouse hallway. No wonder things had gone wrong.

'I'll just go and tuck Gemma up,' Luc called abruptly over his shoulder, as his PA flung open a pair of double doors for him. 'Make yourself comfortable while I do so. Donatello will clear his stuff out, then I'll show you round.'

'I'll come with you,' she said eagerly.

He shot her a cagey look. 'If you must.'

She felt puzzled by his reluctance. Didn't he want her to take a more active part in looking after her daughter? Casting a quick glance about her, she walked across the thick cream carpet towards one of the doors opening off the beautiful sitting room. She had a brief impression of cool toffee-coloured walls, soft honey drapes looped back with enormous gold-fringed tiebacks and a number of comfortable toning sofas. Everything was subtly lit, making the room seem warm and welcoming.

She loved it already. It would be fun looking after Gemma here, she decided happily. In this atmosphere, with no money worries and no neighbours to placate after one of Gemma's tantrums, she'd feel relaxed.

There were no lights on in the small bedroom, but the golden glow from the sitting room relieved the darkness. She could just make out Luc's shadowy figure, standing by the single bed. He was cradling his daughter, rocking her a little in his strong arms and trying to unwrap the soft pink blanket from her small body.

'Just a sec. I'll help you.' She moved forwards as quietly as she could and switched on a bedside lamp. Lovingly she eased the blanket away, her face breaking into a fond smile when Gemma's pyjamas were revealed. 'Teddy bears!' Eyes twinkling with amused affection, she glanced up at Luc from beneath her lashes.

'Her favourite,' he said softly.

He was looking at his child with such tenderness that the breath caught in her throat. This was the Luc she'd known and loved. The soft mouth, lips slightly parted in pleasure to show the white teeth beneath. The affection relaxing every line of his face. The gentleness in the angle of his bent head.

'She means everything to you,' she observed quietly.

'She is my life.'

Passion burned through him, firing the eyes which glowed hot and dark, radiating a heat and energy which awed her. And she felt a pang—whether of wistfulness or envy or resentment, she didn't know. This was her child too. And she'd been denied her for too long.

Please, please, she begged, let Gemma love me!

Never had she wanted that more. At this moment, she believed she could change the situation. Fire seemed to breathe into her too, filling every part of her with a blazing excitement. She could do it. She would do it.

'She's so beautiful.' Ellen reached out to touch her daughter's golden curls in wonder. 'Quite…perfect.' Her voice shattered and she hastily busied herself with reaching out a slim hand and unnecessarily plumping up the pillow.

'Nothing must harm her. Nothing!'

She stared at him, her heart beating wildly. He would kill for his child, she thought, her eyes huge with realisation. She remembered what he'd said, that anyone who hurt Gemma would be hurt in turn. And she felt a little weak at the knees. She understood that fierce protective instinct. She felt the same.

Veiling her eyes to hide the intensity of her own passion, she said as calmly as she could, 'Of course.'

Luc bent and carefully laid Gemma on the bed. Her heavy lashes lifted from her baby-soft cheeks and fluttered open. 'Papà?' she mumbled, catching his big hand in hers.

'Si, sono io,' he whispered, kissing her cheek, and Ellen's heart tumbled over and over in response to his gentleness. 'Go to sleep, sweetheart,' he crooned. 'Papà is here.'

With a contented smile, Gemma closed her eyes and fell asleep again. Ellen lingered, aching to be part of her daughter's life. She'd never been the one to console her child, to offer reassurance and to be trusted implicitly. Whenever Gemma had been upset or hurt, it had been her father she'd turned to.

That would change, Ellen promised herself. And into her mind came a reckless idea. That she should go to live near Luc, and play a more important part in Gemma's daily life. She dismissed the thought. But it kept popping back in her mind as Luc tucked their daughter up.

It could be done. If she dared.

'Goodnight. Sleep well, my angel,' Luc murmured, caressing Gemma's glorious hair adoringly.

She felt like an intruder. And that hurt. As he straightened, he looked over at Ellen's defenceless face, which, she realised too late, must be full of pain and longing. She was aware that her lashes were wet on her cheeks, and her mouth felt moist where she had gently bitten her lip and then released it. And it made her feel vulnerable now that he had caught a glimpse of her most private emotions.

'You should have waited outside,' he muttered gruffly.

'I thought you'd be pleased that I showed some interest,' she returned, refusing to be crushed by him.

'Don't overdo the maternal act. It doesn't fool me.'

Ellen flinched. But she knew that there had been too many years of apparent coolness on her part, and he was perhaps justified in his opinion of her. It was up to her to change it. And she would!

A small smile played about her mouth. 'Just you wait,' she said, her eyes alight with anticipation. 'Things will be very different by the end of this week.'

'I think they will,' he drawled.

Contempt etched his mouth into a hard curve. When he turned back to watch Gemma, his face taut with some inner tension, she was suddenly struck by panic. He'd given her such a strange look. What had it been? Disapproval again? There was definitely a harshness deepening the lines around his mouth.

Perhaps he was worried about trusting his daughter's safety to her—hence his remark warning that no harm must come to her. Gemma was so precious to him that he might be having second thoughts!

'Luc,' she said, touching his arm and desperate to convince him that she could improve her relationship with Gemma. 'I wish you'd relax where I'm concerned. I know we can be friends.'

He jerked his head up, looking at her in disbelief. *'Friends?'*

'Yes!' Disappointed by his reaction, she dragged in a shaky breath and pinned her wet-lashed gaze to his. He had to believe. He just *had* to. 'Friendship is the beginning of love.'

Luc looked even more taken aback. Almost distractedly he picked up Gemma's clothes and put them neatly away. Ellen watched edgily, noticing how unerringly he found the right drawer for her top, her skirt, her socks and underwear. He'd unpacked, she thought enviously. He'd become Gemma's surrogate mother. Would he resent her interference? Did he want to keep Gemma for himself alone, and was that the reason for his stonewalling?

'I want things to change between us,' she said stubbornly. She had a right to Gemma's love. He couldn't take that from her.

'Love… That's what you're aiming for, then?' he said flatly.

Her mouth trembled. He was going to put up some opposition; she could see that in the way he carried his shoulders. 'Why not?' she demanded.

'After all this time—?'

'I refuse to live in the past—'

'Yet it forms the present…and underlies the future.'

'But there have been changes in the situation.' She felt strong enough to cope with risking Gemma's potential rejection now, whereas before she would have gone under.

He pushed his hands in his pockets and eyed her calculatingly, jingling the money in his pocket. 'I have a Cartier watch. Yours comes from a chain store. You work in a supermarket. I run my own business—'

'Luc,' she said, irritated by his unnecessary diversion. 'If my status bothers you, then you might as well know that I am determined not to stay as I am. I will be rich again, but this time I'll make it on my own back.'

'Your frankness amazes me!' he drawled, rocking on his heels.

She heaved a sigh of exasperation. 'I'm trying to make my position clear—'

'On your back,' he prompted.

Her glare should have wilted him. Instead he merely smiled scornfully. 'I realise it's a little early for you to trust me,' she said doggedly, somehow keeping her temper. 'All I'm asking is for you to give me a little while for the relationship to develop. Make allowances for me. I'm sure that, given a chance, I can wipe away all the bad feeling of these past years.'

His eyes glittered. 'That's some ambition. So many bad feelings. So much pain and coldness—'

'I know!' she cried, feeling desperate. He was determined to put obstacles in her way! She willed herself to persevere. 'Anything's possible if you want it enough,' she declared. 'With your help—'

'Me?' He muttered something under his breath.

She caught the word 'pushy', and knew that he'd prefer her to be submissive and adoring. But she'd learnt the hard way that doormats got walked on.

'Yes, you. Stop being hostile.'

He grunted and strolled into the bathroom, where she could see him arranging bath toys neatly on the end of the bath. A family of ducks. A watering can and sieve. A little boat. Ellen gritted her teeth from the pain of exclusion from these simple parental duties.

'And in the place of hostility?' he called, his voice echoing oddly.

She sighed, feeling helpless. He wasn't making this easy! 'Show warmth, a smile, and the occasional...' His bulk filled the doorway. She swallowed, disconcerted by his drowsy gaze. 'Just...be nice! I'll do the rest.'

'I can't wait to see this. Go ahead,' he said with a wave of his hand. 'Be my guest.'

She beamed in delight, her eyes brilliant with emotion.

'You won't regret it,' she said, husky with gratitude that he'd decided to support her attempt. 'I know we'll learn to love one another. I'm determined of that.'

'Love! You want this very badly, don't you?' he mused, his head angled to one side as he contemplated her carefully.

'Of course!' Emboldened, she went over to him. 'You know that. You've seen how I feel, haven't you?' Brief recognition flickered across his eyes and she smiled. He'd noticed the change in her. He knew now that she cared for Gemma. She put a tentative hand on his arm. 'My life would be so different, Luc. My life would be enriched a thousand times over—'

'I have no doubt of that,' he said smoothly, detaching himself. In the low-lit room, the hollows of his cheeks seemed to be accentuated, the line of his jaw sharply angled. 'Have you missed being rich, Ellen?' he asked quietly.

She blinked at the sudden change of subject. And laughed. 'I didn't think so! But when I walked in here and saw the High Life I must confess it seemed very appealing! It's ages since I've been anywhere like this. It's death to the soul to live in unattractive surroundings, Luc,' she told him honestly. 'Luxury bathes the mind and body and warms the heart!' Her expression sobered. 'I'm glad you've done so well,' she said sincerely.

He gave a faint smile. 'It has its disadvantages.'

'Like?' she asked in surprise.

'Some women see me as a meal ticket.'

She winced and looked away from his piercing stare, hating to think of him with other women, gold-diggers or not. A flush spread up her face as she remembered how she'd studied the photographs she'd developed for Gemma, wondering if the two women had made love to Luc.

'I think,' he said in soft, liquid tones, 'it's time for bed.'

Ellen's eyes rounded. 'Oh! Yes,' she said, flustered, going pinker than ever. 'Goodnight, then—'

'Just a minute!'

His hand gripped her shoulder, its warmth sending heat deep into her body. She felt herself tremble, and tensed her muscles in the hope that he hadn't noticed. Unable to bear the pressure of his fingers—because she wanted them to roam all over her—she turned beneath his restraining hand and faced him with a bright, enquiring expression.

'You wanted something?' As soon as she'd said that, she could have beaten herself on the head. How could her mouth betray her like that?

'I'm a man. I always *want*,' he said, making her more nervous than ever. A crooked smile lifted the corner of his mouth as his fingers brushed across her collarbone. 'I also wanted to remind you about Gemma,' he said lazily. 'To say that she sleeps solidly and never wakes, no matter how much noise there is.'

She paused, holding her breath. It seemed he was trying to tell her something. There was nothing innocent about the way he was looking at her. Did he mean...? No! He was just putting her mind at rest, surely?

Deciding to give him the benefit of the doubt, she nodded and headed for the door. 'Lucky her!' she said cheerfully. On an impulse she whirled around and almost collided with him. 'Oh! Sorry!' She took a step back and managed a shaky grin. 'I'm just feeling a bit lightheaded,' she explained, suddenly quite breathless. Her chest seemed to be rising and falling in a highly exaggerated fashion. 'I was going to say that I'm grateful to you for giving me a second chance,' she declared, her throat clogging up suddenly with an overload of emotion.

He cleared his throat, as if he too found it touching that she should be on the brink of reclaiming her child's affection after all this time. Through a watery veil, she gazed affectionately at him. He wasn't so bad. He did have a heart, after all.

'My pleasure, I'm sure. Before we do anything else, I'd better run through room service and my contact numbers with you,' he murmured.

He moved towards her and she hastily side-stepped to make way for him. She took a final glance at her daughter and went after him, hugging herself in delight. Tomorrow, she crowed, she and Gemma would begin again.

After Luc had efficiently prepared her for any emergency, and handed her an alarming amount of cash, Donatello appeared and cheerfully took his leave.

'Meet you at six,' Luc said to his friend, slapping him on the back in affection.

'Six!' she marvelled, when they'd said goodnight and Donatello had left. 'This must be some breakfast meeting! Is it all highly secret?'

Luc's expression became briefly guarded, but then he treated her to one of his dazzling smiles. 'Almost the middle of the night for you, isn't it?' he mused. 'I'm leaving early because I have a fair way to drive for my meeting. Reminds me of my lorry driving days when I got up at five. Remember?'

Somehow she managed to smile too. 'Ghastly.' But her mind had winged back to the early days when he'd woken and made love to her, leaving her sprawled languidly on the bed and feeling sated and loved.

'Don't worry. I won't disturb you.'

From the way he looked, she wondered if he'd remembered those days too. Dragging her gaze from his soft mouth, she said awkwardly, 'What a relief!'

Luc studied her with his penetrating stare. 'You can get me on my mobile any time, remember. Gemma's welfare comes before anyone and everything. Got that? Contact me if you're at all concerned or you need advice.'

She couldn't fault him on his devotion. A plaintive little wail nestled in her head. Why hadn't he given her that much attention when they were first married? Why hadn't their relationship, their love, come first, before work? Ruthlessly she stopped herself from whinging about the past and concentrated on the future. Her eyes began to sparkle.

'I think I'll manage. Oh, Luc, we're going to have such fun! I can't wait for you to find out all the surprises I'm planning!'

There was a slight change in the way he stood. A tension which hadn't been there before, an electricity in the atmosphere. There was an answering tightness in her chest, and she knew her breasts were ripening beneath his hungry stare.

Her toes curled in her shoes and she swayed when he eased his tie loose and undid his top shirt button. It had always been one of the sexiest things he did and this time was no exception. He looked so incredibly handsome, she thought hazily. His mouth had become deliciously pliable and ready to be kissed...

'Shall we have a night-cap?' he murmured, the cadences of his voice slipping silkily along her sensitised nervous system.

Tempting though that sounded, she knew that it would be unwise to accept. He was back in macho mood again, and definitely giving her a sexual invitation.

'I think I'll turn in, thanks,' she said, and calmly—how did she do it?—pushed her shaky legs towards the bedroom Donatello had vacated.

Behind her she heard the chink of a glass. Luc was comforting himself with a whisky. Good! Her hand closed on the doorknob and suddenly she froze. He was walking swiftly towards her.

'Let's check you have everything, shall we?' he suggested, clearly intending to follow her into the bedroom.

'All I need is a bed,' she said in jerky little spurts. Before he misconstrued that stupid remark, she pushed the door open, intending to say goodnight to him and to shut it quickly before he took another step.

But Luc's hand was on hers and he was right behind

her, his body exuding warmth and that knee-weakening
male smell. She had to move forwards into the room or
be plastered against his chest and loins. Her back quivered
at the very thought, giving an unintentional wiggle to her
hips which she quickly brought under severe control
again.

'It's a double bed. I hope that meets with your ap-
proval,' he said quietly.

'Perfect.' Fear made her babble inanely. 'I can thrash
around all I like, can't I?' She groaned. Her big mouth!

To her alarm, he closed the door behind them, then
strode past her and into the *en suite* bathroom. 'Toothbrush, paste, flannel and bathrobe…here,' he called, while
she remained rooted to the spot and trying to overcome
her nerves. 'Obviously shoe-cleaning stuff, the usual
things. You can ring the housekeeper if there's anything
else you need.' He reappeared, smiling and studying her
from beneath half-closed lashes. He took a swig of
whisky and made her stomach contract by briefly touching his lips with the tip of his tongue.

'B-brilliant,' she husked and dropped her gaze. 'Night,
then.'

'I'm glad you're more…together,' he said softly, determined, it seemed, to prolong his visit. 'Donatello said
you'd been very remote…well…"lifeless and indifferent" was how he expressed it.' He gave a short laugh.
'You're hardly that now.'

'I told you.' Pointedly she switched on the bedside
lamp. 'I've been ill.'

'And now you're back to normal,' he mused. 'As beautiful as ever. More lovely, perhaps.'

'Thanks.' This was hurting. He was making a play for
her and all she could think was that it was too late. The
marriage was dead. 'Luc…'

She made the mistake of looking at him. Their eyes
met and in that instant she saw the rawness of his longing.
Astonishingly, it wasn't a lust which had been encouraged

by her figure-hugging top and skirt, or by her recent display of nakedness in the art class.

Her eyes widened and softened as it dawned on her: he felt the same sense of loss. There was a sadness in his eyes, a deep hunger for the love they'd once felt for one another. And she felt that too, from the bottom of her heart, her emotions spilling into every corner of her body in an unstoppable flood.

'Ellen,' he said in an appealing, gravelly voice.

'*Luc.*'

Or that was what she'd meant to say, loving the sound of his name. She'd shaped the word but her throat was so choked with sweetly poignant feelings that no sound had emerged. Being wistful about the past didn't mean he cared, she told herself severely. Anyone could mourn happier times.

As if in slow motion, he put down his glass with studied deliberation, his gaze never leaving hers. She couldn't move and neither, it seemed, could he.

If she tried, she could stop him now, with a word or a gesture. It would be so easy. A haughty tilt of her head, a snappy remark... But while he looked at her like that she couldn't bear to betray what was between them by pretending that she didn't care, that she didn't want him to touch her and kiss her... Her head rolled back and a small moan whispered imperceptibly through her lips.

But he'd heard it in the stillness of the room. She closed her eyes when he walked with maddening slowness towards her. In the hushed silence she sensed his nearness and the soft sound of his breathing, and registered how fast it was—as rushed and as strangled as hers. There was nothing she could do but remain waiting helplessly. This situation had been inevitable from the moment she'd heard his voice on the telephone; she realised that now in the deep secrecy of her heart.

Because she might hate him, but she certainly still loved him.

And yet as the silence lengthened, and the tensions in her body drove her crazy with suppressed desire, she remembered her vow that he'd never touch her or humiliate her again.

Her eyes snapped open wide. 'N-no, Luc,' she whispered, hoarse with the pain of denial.

Too little, too late. His eyes had become drowsy, and his hot mouth descended swiftly to sear hers with a punishing kiss which took her by surprise and bore her backwards forcibly, till she fell so hard onto the bed that her breath left her body and only excitement and a delicious anticipation remained.

A storm of kisses rained on her lips and every inch of her face. He wasn't allowing her time to think—every part of her seemed to be focused on the fierce hunger of his mouth…and now, fatally, his marauding hands.

One had slid to her thigh, where his fingers stroked in a monotonous, maddening rhythm. One was stealing millimetre by millimetre beneath her cropped top, and suddenly, before she knew what she was doing, she was returning his kisses, her mind and body assailed by physical and emotional sensations which blocked out her ability to be sensible and call a halt to his assault.

Her hands caressed his hair where it curled just above his collar. Her head was thrown back and his mouth was exploring her slender throat with gentle kisses which were unbelievably tantalising in their promise. She drew in a shuddering breath. He was sliding his hand to the underside of her breast, and at the same time as his lips encircled the painfully hard nipple she felt the touch of his fingers on the inside of her thigh.

Perfect timing. He'd always known how to drive her wild, how to pile sensation on sensation till she was completely incoherent and frantic for more.

She tensed every muscle. She had to stop him. This was madness…

'*Le piace questo?*' he murmured throatily.

She bit her lip to stop herself from blurting out the truth. Yes, she liked it. Adored it. Wanted more.

No one had touched her there except Luc, and the smooth slide of his fingers was evoking painfully wonderful memories in her mind and body even as they aroused her beyond all control.

'Ahhh…' she groaned on an outrush of breath, as he probed more deeply.

'E questo…e quello…qui…la…'

And this, and that, here, there… Yes! Yes! she wanted to cry. He was driving her insane, kissing her, touching her, whispering seductively in that infuriatingly sensual Italian till she was no longer in her right mind but overwhelmed with the need for satisfaction. But not at any cost. If all he wanted was sex, then he could go elsewhere, she thought miserably.

Her hands pushed at his shoulders and he looked down at her in surprise. 'I don't think—'

'Perfect. No thinking. Just action,' he said, cradling her breast in his hand and stroking it maddeningly with his forefinger. And all she could think of at that moment was…just a little closer, a fraction nearer and he would be relieving the ache within.

'No, Luc, I mean—'

'This isn't just sex, is it?' he said rawly, tasting her arching throat with an intensity of passion which brought her close to groaning aloud. 'This is more than that. Much more…'

The truth was there, in the torment in his eyes and the shakiness of his voice. It showed in the desperate tension of his mouth and the faint frown disturbing the smoothness of his forehead, as if he feared she'd draw away.

Her heart leapt. She could hardly believe it… Every look, every gesture, told her that he was yearning for the love they'd once shared. Her thoughts whirled, thinking the unthinkable but too scared to allow herself that luxury.

A trembling mass of hope, she felt his finger testing

the softness of her jutting lower lip. He slipped his finger between her teeth, and without being able to help herself she nibbled and then suckled it gently, her eyes closed in a bittersweet anguish when he withdrew it.

She jerked when he found new places to tantalise, her body reacting to his touch till it almost vibrated with pleasure. Each bone in her shoulder claimed his attention. Each muscle grew soft and giving from the trail of his kisses.

But still she held back. Go by your instincts, her friends had said. That was all you could trust. And she'd seen signs of longing. Perhaps…the hint of something more. Desperately she tried to think. The risk was huge. But so was the gain.

'I've wanted this for so long,' he murmured into her hair, kissing her feathery curls from the top of her head to where they nestled at the nape of her neck.

Uncertainly she took his face between her hands and studied him with solemn, anxious eyes. The ache to love him surged up and caught her unawares, making a sob break from her lips. And Luc's expression of pained, tender concern convinced her. He did care!

Gently she touched her lips to his. 'Me too,' she breathed. 'Make love to me!'

He threw his head back and groaned. Then he kissed her so hard that her lips felt bruised and swollen when he lifted his mouth. But she didn't give a damn. She felt the same urgent violence, the same frantic need, and moaned in anguish as his long fingers fumbled with the clasp on her skirt.

He dragged it down over her hips. She felt the warmth of his mouth on her firm stomach, and then his fingers had torn away her briefs.

'God!' he groaned. 'I can't believe how much I want you!'

And then he was kissing her—as though he was starved of a woman's mouth, almost, she thought in hazy confusion, as if he was punishing himself—or her. Their bodies writhed together and she connived with him to remove her soft cotton top till it freed her tumbling breasts.

'Oh, Luc, that's wonderful!' she whispered, when he suckled each one with deep concentration. Her heart was near to breaking when she gazed at his rapt face. Tenderly she touched his hair and stroked the smooth forehead.

And then his hands were all but crushing her slender shoulders as his gaze avidly raked her entire body, leaving every inch of it tingling with sensation. She lifted up her arms to him, arching her body in unconscious demand because she couldn't bear to wait any longer.

Luc dragged in a strangled breath, and suddenly the weight of his body was covering hers, and a huge rush of air left her lungs as she groaned in pleasure and relief, revelling in the feeling of joy and possession, the firmness of him, the fierce heat of his breath on her neck.

He had returned to her. It was a wonderful moment, far beyond her wildest dreams. Fantasies spun madly in her head, heightening her love and the urgency of her desire. She, Luc and Gemma. They would all be together. Unbelievable! Ecstatic, she wrapped her arms around him tightly, using all her strength to hug him close.

'Take my clothes off,' he whispered, lifting himself up a little.

She struggled for a moment or two, furious that his buttons wouldn't come free. Luc smiled and merely ripped the shirt apart, flinging it away and lowering himself again so they just touched, skin to skin, breast to breast. They both released a shaky breath at that moment, and she felt a lurch of wild delight that his heart should be thudding so erratically.

The way he kissed her, the way he touched and caressed and murmured to her were all music to her soul. It was as if there had been no ill will between them. And she believed in that moment that they would never part again and her heart lurched with an indescribable joy.

Hungry for him to claim her again, aching to be part of him, she reached down to undo his waistband and ease his zip. Then he was naked at last. His flesh on hers. She held her breath in a turmoil of swirling emotion.

Ellen's eyes misted. Everything would be all right. She just knew it.

'Take me,' she whispered, overcome with love. 'I need you so much!'

Pain slashed silver paths across his eyes as he stared down at her. And then he buried his head in her neck, lifted his hips and drove into her. She bucked in shock, but almost immediately gasped in pleasure as his long, slow strokes began their magic.

He was desperate too. The fierceness of his lovemaking matched hers as every inch of his body tautened and he began to move with increasing speed and intensity. He muttered angrily into her neck, but she didn't understand what he was saying. Only half her mind registered all this. The rest of her was flying, soaring with her heart and soul because she was with Luc and he wanted her again.

He rolled her over with grim intent and she straddled him, teasing him with the sway of her hips and her breasts. He seemed insatiable. Heat was building within her. She was losing all sense of reality as his hands slithered all over her body and his tongue slicked her nipples into painful, erotic dark peaks.

He hardly knew what he was doing. Couldn't look at her. The pleasure was intense. He kept his eyes tightly shut as he explored her whole body, his fingers and mouth tasting, kissing and caressing, till he felt her breathing shorten and that incredibly sensuous tightening around him, the spasms of imminent surrender which he'd been waiting for.

He flipped her onto her back again, then with a huge effort of will, he hesitated. She cried out, as he knew she would.

'Please, Luc! *Please!*' she whimpered, crushing her lips to his mouth in her hopelessness. Her tongue seduced him, her body lured him as she used all the tricks she could. For a long time he let her torment him. Till he could take it no longer.

And then he moved, unable to hold back, fast, hard, stabbing. His heart pounded uncomfortably in his chest, every blood vessel in his body engorged and throbbing. She was a witch, he thought dazedly. A beautiful, wickedly sexy Jezebel...

He was losing consciousness. Her body was claiming his, driving him to the wildest, most intense and prolonged orgasm he'd ever known. The next few moments were blurred by pleasure, by her cries and his, their mouths searching for one another, hands, fingers clutching and squeezing as they rolled around the bed in a hot tumble of resisting flesh and wave after wave of sensation gripped his body.

Slowly he came to. For a while he lay there, panting and amazed. Small tremors assailed him, making him jerk as if they were aftershocks following the earthquake that had occurred. And Ellen trembled too, her very skin rippling with the tension and flexion of her muscles. He gathered her close and waited for them both to be still, but his mind had become sharp and active.

This wasn't what he'd planned at all. He'd succeeded in the first part of his scheme. But at one hell of a price.

CHAPTER FIVE

ELLEN felt blissfully peaceful. The future stretched ahead like a long, golden path. Too drained to speak, she surrendered to the pleasure of being in Luc's arms. But almost as soon as she began to nestle into him he began detaching himself, and then he rolled away.

Feeling deprived, she stretched languorously, sighing in the hope that he'd change his mind. Despite the ripples in his muscles which suggested he'd heard her invitation, he began to gather up his clothes—for all the world like a casual lover who'd only wanted her for sex.

It had been more than that! He'd said so! Alarmed, she sat up, the sheet falling completely away from her naked body.

'Don't go,' she whispered in a soft caress.

'Stop looking at me like that!' he muttered thickly.

'Like what, Luc?' she purred in a pretence of innocence, reassured and delighted by his immediate physical response.

'As if you want more.'

She smiled, seduction definitely on her mind. 'Is it a crime for me to want everything you have to offer?' she asked huskily, wriggling over to the edge of the bed and stroking the firm skin of his thigh. For a second he stood very still, allowing her to trace the line of his muscles, his whole body quivering beneath her wandering fingers. Awed, she looked up at him. His eyes were closed, his expression ecstatic. 'You want me,' she breathed, tormenting him by crawling her forefinger closer and closer to the top of his leg.

'All the time.'

Surprise, delight and desire rushed through her at the force of his growled reply. All the time! She could hardly breathe for joy. 'Then stay,' she whispered, seized with an uncontrollable happiness. 'Stay!' she cried with a joyful laugh. 'It's been so long, Luc—'

'No.' He stepped back, leaving her with her arm outstretched in mid-air. His mouth twisted in a strange smile. 'I learnt long ago as a child that I couldn't have everything I wanted.'

She nodded, her eyes solemn. 'I know. But that was then. Now—'

'Now I must also deny myself. I have an early start. I must go. I need some sleep.'

'You can sleep here,' she offered, longing for him to stay the night with her. 'Lie with me,' she murmured persuasively, allowing her eyes to tell him what pleasure that would give her.

He shook his head, then leaned forwards and kissed her lingeringly on the mouth. 'You don't think we'd sleep, do you? You're far too provocative,' he whispered softly in her ear. 'I'd be a wreck in the morning.'

'Oh, Luc!' she mumbled in disappointment.

But she caressed the hard line of his jaw, a feeling of tenderness touching her heart when she discovered how hard he was clenching his teeth. He was alarmingly strong-willed. It was more than obvious he still wanted her. Taking pity on him, she deposited a kiss on his chin and flopped back on the bed, obligingly covering herself. There would be other days—many of them.

'Go on, then!' she said with an understanding smile..

Averting his eyes, he scraped a hand through his hair in shaky relief. 'Enjoy your day with Gemma,' he said hoarsely, doing his best not to look at her. 'Give her an early evening tea and I'll be back to put her to bed.'

'I'll look forward to that.' Out of the blue, her eyes began to swim with happy tears. 'Luc, you can't imagine what this has meant to me—'

'I think I can,' he rasped. Perhaps because he was trying not to weaken, he moved sharply away from the bed and strode across the room as if demons were after him. 'Night. Sleep well,' he added, clipping each word short. And let himself out.

She smiled to herself, flattered that he'd found it hard to leave her. Luc had wanted her in every way, not just sexually. And their lovemaking had been mind-blowing. They were meant for one another—he couldn't fail to realise that.

With a sigh of deep contentment, she went to take a shower. Then, warm and glowing with happiness, she straightened the untidy bed and snuggled down, falling fast asleep within seconds of her head touching the downy pillow. She slept undisturbed the whole night through for the first time in years.

Light filtered through a gap in the curtains, announcing that it was morning, but she lay still, enjoying the memories of the night before. And then her door opened. Blearily she rolled over to see Gemma's small form in her teddy bear pyjamas.

'Hello, there!' Ellen said in sleepy delight.

Before she had a chance to invite Gemma over for a hug, the child had spun around on her heel and disappeared. Shaken by this unexpected response, Ellen leapt out of bed and flung on the hotel towelling robe to discover that Gemma was in the sitting room, telephone in hand, calmly ordering breakfast to be brought to the suite.

'Orange, yes. And toast. Thank you.' She put the phone down.

'How grown up you are! Have you ordered for me?' Ellen asked warmly.

Gemma didn't falter on her way to her bedroom. 'No.'

Flinching, Ellen quickly rallied, grabbing the phone and putting in her own order before appearing casually at her daughter's open door. 'It's lovely to see you,' she said, coming forward and impulsively catching hold of

Gemma's small hand. It was snatched away and Ellen was treated to a black scowl so like her father's that her heart lurched. 'You...did want to stay with me, didn't you?' she asked nervously, fearing for a brief, disloyal moment that Luc might have been lying to her.

Gemma was sullenly collecting clothes from various drawers. 'I want my *papà.*'

She smiled understandingly. Gemma had forgotten. 'He's gone to work, sweetheart. Remember? He did tell you last night,' Ellen explained gently. 'He said we could go shopping. Shall we get you something nice?' She groaned inwardly at her stupidity. The child would hardly want something horrible!

But Gemma shot her a glance which indicated her interest had been caught. Her curls bounced as she nodded solemnly, and then she turned her back and began to dress.

Ellen watched, feeling incredibly deflated. OK, perhaps she'd been over-optimistic in thinking that Gemma would rush into her arms with a cry of 'Mother!', but Luc had led her to believe that Gemma had had a change of heart. She'd imagined all kinds of things, from an exchange of shy glances to instant hugs. It seemed, however, that nothing had changed.

Gemma turned, balancing her slender, strong little body skilfully as she stood on one leg and pulled on a pair of teddy bear knickers. Ellen gave a small gasp, her attention riveted by the yellowing bruise on Gemma's lower back.

In an instant she was kneeling beside her daughter in concern. 'That looks awful! You poor darling! How did you do it?' she murmured sympathetically. Ellen's fingers lightly touched the discoloured area and her daughter suddenly went as stiff as a board. 'It's all right. I won't hurt you,' Ellen assured her hastily.

But Gemma had begun to tremble with fear and all Ellen's instincts told her that something was wrong. An icy coldness chased down her spine and her heart began to pump rapidly as she thought of several possibilities—then hastily dismissed them from her mind as too awful to contemplate.

It was something simple. 'What happened? A fall at school?' she asked gently, managing to conceal her anxiety. Perhaps Gemma hadn't understood. *'La scuola?'* she prompted.

Gemma's face paled. *'Sono caduto giù per le scale,'* she mumbled, doing a little mime.

'You fell down the stairs?' Ellen repeated in relief, feeling ridiculous for imagining anything more sinister. 'Oh, that's awful! It must have hurt.' Ellen smiled tenderly at Gemma's puzzled face and realised she needed to elaborate. 'Ouch!' she cried, rubbing her back ruefully. 'Yes?'

Ignoring her again, Gemma ran back into the sitting room. Ellen sighed and went to phone the supermarket to say that she wouldn't be in that week.

It was, she thought wryly, going to be quite a day.

In fact, it turned out to be a mixed success. After a morning's shopping—which they both enjoyed despite Gemma's pretence to the contrary—they made a visit to the Children's Costume Museum. The highlight was when Gemma joined a group of children trying on Victorian clothes.

Here, Ellen was just one of the other mums, helping her child to struggle into one of the crinolines and watching in helpless laughter as Gemma practised sitting down without displaying the long lace pantaloons.

And along with the other parents she watched with sentimental affection as her grandly dressed daughter swept into the hall later and took part in a pretend banquet, with ice cream and crisps as the unlikely staple diet.

'Which is your kiddie?' a mother beside her whispered.

Ellen's heart swelled. 'The one in the green feathered hat telling that sweet little footman she wants some wine,' she replied with a chuckle.

'She's lovely. I picked her out at once,' the mother said. 'And that sweet little footman's my little toad of a son!'

They chatted for a while. Ellen enjoyed every moment of the casual conversation. It was the first time she'd watched her child from the sidelines with other parents and she made the most of it.

Gemma chatted excitedly afterwards, sometimes lapsing into Italian, which fascinated everybody till she said that her *papà* came from Napoli.

'Naples,' Ellen had explained.

'Napoli,' repeated Gemma, and everyone laughed.

But Ellen had seen the set of her daughter's stubborn mouth and could have kicked herself for being so tactless. When she reached out her hand for Gemma to take, it was not only ignored—as it had been all day—but irritably brushed aside.

'They're so independent at that age, aren't they?' sighed the mother to whom she'd spoken earlier. 'My Tom makes me walk a few steps behind him on the way to school!'

Ellen laughed, but she felt tears prick her eyes. It took a while for common sense to reassert itself. She mustn't expect miracles. They'd had a good day. That was the first step.

And now they were both waiting impatiently for Luc to come home, peering out of the window in the hope they might see him arrive in the street far below. But the first inkling they had that he was on his way was when he flung open the door and stood there, looking immaculately groomed, despite his long day, and wonderfully, aggressively masculine in a perfectly tailored navy and chalk-striped suit.

'Papà!' squealed Gemma excitedly, launching herself in a flurry of crisp pink skirts towards the door. She flung herself into mid-air, where Luc caught her expertly and swung her around.

'*Ciao!* How are you, my beautiful princess?' he cried, laughing and kissing her heartily. 'Oh, you look wonderful! This is a new dress!' He put her down, beaming at her. 'Turn around. Yes. Very nice.'

Gemma began chattering in Italian. Luc crouched down adoringly, completely wrapped up in his daughter.

Or…was he? Ellen, standing awkwardly, uncertainly, by the window, saw him shoot her a sidelong glance or two from his warm chocolate eyes. Emboldened, she came forwards, still in the hipster jeans and close-fitting white shirt she'd worn that day.

'Hello, Luc. You must be tired,' she said sympathetically, longing to fling herself into his arms too.

He rose, almost warily. 'Hello, Ellen,' he said, with a rather strained enthusiasm. She felt herself flinch. More gently he added, 'I am.' For a moment he hesitated and then, to her confused delight, he leaned forwards and saluted her, Italian-style, with a triple kiss.

Gemma's chatter stopped abruptly, and they both looked down at her in amused surprise. She treated Ellen to a long and searching perusal, as though seeing her for the first time.

Not knowing what to make of this, Ellen broke the tense silence. 'We must tell your *papà* what we did today,' she said lightly.

'Ah, yes. You had a good day?' Luc enquired, picking up the cue, his face immediately suffused with smiles.

Gemma thought for a moment, finding the right words. 'We went shopping,' she announced, unable to hide her glee.

He pretended to groan. 'Then I have no money! You have taken all my money!'

She giggled. He bent down again and she solemnly removed his jacket, taking it and hanging it carefully on the back of a chair. Then she undid his tie, slid it off and fumbled with his top shirt button, her face a study in concentration.

Ellen's heart turned over. This was a well-rehearsed ritual which had evolved over a long time. Her daughter had been doing this every evening, caring for her father and showing her love for him in the solemn, self-important manner in which she carried out her duties.

But soon, Ellen promised herself, she would be part of these rituals. Luc and she would grow closer and Gemma would see how happy they were together and they would become a real family. Her eyes shone with happiness as she watched the two of them, a blissful smile on her ecstatic face.

The shirt button successfully released, Luc proffered his cheek and received two smacking kisses. He hugged Gemma and swept her up in his arms, nuzzling her tummy and making her laugh while Ellen watched enviously.

'Now,' he said, sitting on the sofa and perching Gemma on his thigh. 'Tell me—am I a poor man?' he asked with an expression of exaggerated fear, his knees knocking together alarmingly.

Trying to keep her balance, Gemma collapsed in fits of giggles as Luc acted the fool. He was a wonderful father, Ellen thought, bursting into laughter when he pretended to turn out his pockets only to find them empty. Gemma forced his fists open and pointed reprovingly to the coins he'd been concealing. The teasing went on.

Ellen knew it wasn't for her benefit. Sometimes he seemed to have forgotten her existence. Gemma certainly had, ignoring her as if she wasn't even there. Ellen realised she'd have to tread very carefully and not intrude on their private little games.

'She's still excluding you,' said Luc thoughtfully sometime later, when they both had showered and changed and were enjoying a simple supper in the suite.

She hadn't minded not eating out somewhere exotic; it meant they could be together in private. Dreamily she smiled, her eyes bright with pleasure.

'When you're around she sees no one else. But we had fun, even if she won't admit it. At the museum, I think she liked being a maid and cleaning the silver best! You're missing an employment opportunity there!'

Luc smiled faintly, picked up her hand from where it rested on the table and kissed her fingers, his long lashes hiding the expression in his eyes.

'I'm glad everything went to your satisfaction,' he murmured.

Turning her hand, he pressed his lips to the hollow of her palm and she gave a little gasp. It took only a glance or a touch from him and her whole body came alive, she thought in wonder. He looked up then, his eyebrow lifting in enquiry, as if he expected to have a more detailed account than the one she and Gemma had given him earlier.

But she wanted to hear him speak, to listen to his honeyed tones and let his voice seep through her pores to her very bones. 'I'm making progress,' she assured him, her lips parting in response to the movement of his thumb on the silken skin of her wrist.

'You think so?'

'Yes. I'm determined to get where I want,' she told him, deliciously aware that his dark eyes were fixed on the deep cleft between her breasts. 'How about your day?' she asked huskily. 'Good meeting?'

'Fine. You look particularly lovely tonight, Ellen. Your dress is very flattering,' he replied with a smooth and practised charm.

She beamed and admired it too. It was of a beautifully cut buttermilk silk and slid over her figure as if it had been poured on. The neckline was a little daring, but flattered her shoulders and exposed the soft swell of her breasts. Which his gaze returned to with flattering regularity.

She had taken care not to buy too much, choosing only sufficient clothes not to embarrass Luc while she was staying at the hotel. But she thought she'd tease him, Gemma-style.

'Glad you like it. You paid a fortune for it!' she said with an impudent little chuckle.

He smiled lazily and put his napkin on the table. 'Bedtime, I think.'

A quiver ran through her. He studied her flushed face and then let his gaze drift down to the rise and fall of her breasts. The message was clear. Blatant desire showed more forcibly with every breath he took. Drawn to him like a magnet, she rose and went over to him.

Her hands rested briefly on his broad shoulders, feeling the strength of him beneath the fine cloth. Then she took his face in the cradle of her two palms and bent to kiss him lingeringly on the mouth.

He tasted sweet. Starved of him for a whole day, she crushed his mouth with hers and found herself in his arms. Her kisses grew more passionate as his hands radiated heat where they rested on her back and waist.

She wanted him to touch her breasts but he stayed almost impassive, accepting her kisses, holding her and breathing heavily, but otherwise making no other response. Recognising this as a sex game they'd played long ago, she took up the challenge and went for the full seduction she knew he adored.

'Kiss me,' she urged, teasing the beautiful V of his mouth with her tongue. 'Kiss me!' she whispered, writhing her body against his. Hooking up a questing finger, she slid one strap of her dress from her shoulder. 'Touch me.' She took his hand from her waist and raised it so that it rested on her half-naked breast. 'Touch me there.' Her tongue slid between his teeth and tentatively explored the moistness of his mouth while her hand crept beneath his shirt.

Luc drew back from her intimate kiss, breathing heavily. 'Bed,' he rasped.

She let a slow and sensual smile light her drugged eyes.

'Whatever you want,' she whispered, intoxicated by her success.

'So you don't mind?' he asked huskily, pushing his chair back and standing up so that she was forced to scrabble for her balance.

Now she was confused. 'Mind?' she said, blinking stupidly. Of course she didn't mind!

'If I go to bed,' he said. 'I'm absolutely whacked.'

Ellen gaped and felt the rise of colour settle on her burning cheeks as if she'd been scalded. For a moment she wanted to crawl under the table in shame.

'Not at all!' she lied over-energetically, appalled at how badly she'd misread his needs.

She could have sworn he'd given her a come-on signal. Oh, this was terrible! All she could do was bluff it out. Seeing his eyes flicker down, she hastily grabbed her strap and pulled it back into place.

He seemed amused, and she cringed when he drawled, 'I enjoyed the after-dinner entertainment. I can't wait to know what you've laid on for me tomorrow night.'

She had to say something light and amusing. Plucking from the ether the first thing that occurred to her, she presented him with a high-wattage smile and decided on a joke.

'Tomorrow you get a can-can. This evening I thought I ought to thank you nicely for your cash gift in the time-honoured way,' she returned, with a jauntiness she didn't feel.

Luc's hot dark eyes gleamed with sardonic amusement. 'I accept your performance as a down payment,' he murmured drolly. 'Goodnight, Ellen.'

He was going! She wanted a moment longer...a little more of his time... 'Will I—we—see you in the morning?' she asked, her voice high and far too casual to be believed.

'Sure.' He smiled faintly when she looked pleased. 'Providing you get up at six.'

Her face fell. 'When will you be back?' she asked, horribly reluctant to see him leave. She felt like a teenage girl, mooning over her first boyfriend! she thought crossly. Of course he was tired. He'd had a long day.

'Late.'

'Oh,' she said in a small voice.

Luc cleared his throat. 'Ellen,' he said quietly, 'this is a delicate negotiation I'm working on. It's taking all my concentration and I need my wits about me.'

'Yes,' she said, nodding vigorously. 'I do understand.' And, knowing she had no right to detain him or make him feel guilty about working so long, she managed a shaky smile of apology. 'Gemma will be disappointed,' she said, 'but I'll make her bedtime as enjoyable as possible.' There were compensations, she thought. She'd be the one who tucked Gemma up in bed tomorrow night.

'Keep her up for me,' he said, immediately robbing her of that one consolation. 'Look, I really don't expect you to act as unpaid nanny twenty-four hours a day—'

'I'm Gemma's mother! That's what mothers do!' she cried, hurt that he saw her as an outsider.

'Yes. But you need a break. Donatello will be back around four tomorrow afternoon and he'll take over Gemma for you so you can have time to yourself. No, please—I insist,' he said, when she opened her mouth to object. 'He adores her. He might be a confirmed bachelor, but he does know how to entertain children. He'll probably amuse her for a while then persuade her to take a nap so she can see me in the evening. Right,' he said decisively, leaving her no grounds for discussing the arrangement. 'I'm off, before I fall asleep on my feet.' And he gave a perfunctory smile then strode quickly to his room.

She couldn't help noticing that he didn't look half as tired as he claimed. He still brimmed with energy, and an intense sexual electricity radiated from his body, drawing her towards him like a dog on a lead, she thought gloomily.

The door shut behind him and she slumped into a chair. She'd made a fool of herself. She really mustn't throw herself at him! Wishing she didn't feel so ridiculously rejected, she gritted her teeth and took herself off to bed with a good book. But it wasn't good enough, and she couldn't get back into the story at all.

Some time in the night, when she was lying awake and crossly counting an endless line of sheep, she heard her door open. And, to her immense joy, Luc slipped into bed with her.

'Luc!' she whispered in delight.

'I couldn't sleep,' he muttered, almost crossly, and enveloped her with his arms and body.

She smiled happily. 'I've just the thing for that!' she purred.

He had left her bed by the time she woke up. Ellen stretched like a satisfied cat, her body intensely alive from Luc's passionate loving. Wandering around the suite, it didn't take her long to realise that he'd actually left for work. That alone bothered her—it was only five o'clock.

It seemed that he hadn't changed his habits, and this worried her. Their relationship had foundered before because he felt obliged to work all hours. And it couldn't be good for Gemma if her father was rarely home.

It was a problem they must solve, she mused, making a cup of coffee, or their relationship would be no different from before. She'd progressed too far to return to being a sex object and a wife and mother. Her expectations included companionship and a sharing of their lives. They'd never be a real family if Luc insisted on playing the macho Italian patriarch while she was forced into being a carbon copy of his *mamma*.

One thing at a time, she told herself. First she must win Gemma over.

To that end, she treated her daughter to a morning by the Round Pond in Kensington Gardens, flying the kite they'd purchased the day before. Again, the outing went well, with the two of them laughing in sheer exhilaration as the kite soared and swooped and performed amazing acrobatic feats in the brisk wind.

Glowing from the fresh air and the sense of freedom that she always felt after kite-flying, Ellen rushed Gemma off to Charing Cross by taxi to buy tricks from the Magic Shop. And before Donatello arrived they practised the tricks to show to Luc that evening.

Oddly, Luc's PA seemed edgy when he called to take Gemma away. Ellen noticed immediately that he wouldn't meet her eyes. Assuming he might have an inkling of what had happened between Luc and herself, she took pity on his embarrassment and left him to take the excited Gemma downstairs.

It was nice to have a break. It pleased her that Luc had thought to arrange for her to have some time to herself. She relaxed in a long, luxurious bath and pampered herself for him, using some of the body creams in the bathroom and then choosing her dress with great care.

She had just slithered into a wicked-but-simple black designer dress, and was wondering nervously if it was too figure-hugging and too short—it reached barely mid-thigh—when she heard the squeals and laughter which must surely herald Luc's arrival with Gemma. She assumed that he must have stopped off at Donatello's room and collected his daughter.

Her body began to tremble. 'Idiot!' she muttered at the huge-eyed glamour-puss in the mirror.

Arrested, she stared at herself, amazed that a well-cut dress with just the right depth of black could do such a lot for her figure and skin. Or was it that Luc was waiting out there? She grinned. Who cared? Her eyes danced. This would be a night he'd never forget—providing, she reminded herself sternly, he wasn't too shattered.

Taking several deep breaths, she wandered out, and was gratified by Luc's reaction.

After a double take, he came straight to her, kissed her three times and whispered wickedly in her ear, 'You do know how to seduce a man, Ellen!'

'Who, me?' she murmured, trying to be wide-eyed and innocent.

'Can't imagine how you're going to do the can-can in that!' he teased.

'I'm very resourceful,' she said airily.

Luc smiled faintly. 'I'm beginning to discover that.' And then he raised his voice and said loudly, 'I believe a magician is waiting to give me a show!'

Ellen caught Gemma's eye and nodded. The little girl ran to get her tricks and set them up solemnly on a small table. Then, tongue protruding in concentration, Gemma waved her magic wand and began the routine she'd rehearsed so carefully.

Proudly, Ellen acknowledged that her daughter was very bright. She'd mastered the simple techniques involved and was putting on a good show. Ellen watched the finale with fond tears in her eyes as Gemma solemnly pulled silk scarves from her mouth in a series of dramatic flourishes and Luc obligingly let his jaw drop and uttered cries of complete amazement.

This was a day she would cherish for the rest of her life.

After the kite-flying, Gemma had actually let her hold her hand. They had laughed together and giggled furtively like naughty schoolgirls whilst they'd tried that afternoon to perfect each trick.

Remembering this, she felt a huge tension in her chest, as if it was filled with so much love that it might burst. Now she had the people she adored close again, she'd never let them go. They all belonged together. She smiled fondly at them both and let out a deep sigh.

It went unheard, fortunately. Gemma was bowing and

Luc had risen to applaud long and loud. The magician gave up her well-deserved curtain call and flung herself at her audience, who held her lovingly close to his heart while Ellen blew her nose and muttered something about starting a cold.

As a reward, Luc read to Gemma for a while, stroking her hair and speaking in his beautiful musical voice which raised the hairs on the back of Ellen's neck. She just sat opposite them watching adoringly, a stupid smile permanently on her face. What more could she ask of life? she wondered blissfully. These two held the key to her heart and her happiness and she basked in the glow of deep contentment which enfolded her.

'Would you like to stay up late, sweetheart?' Luc asked, brushing a bouncing curl from Gemma's small face. 'I am going out this evening. I thought 'Tello could stay with you. You could both play Snakes and Ladders, then watch the video I brought home. Yes?'

She looked sulky. 'I love you, Papà,' she said, twirling the short dark hair in front of his ear, clearly reluctant to let her father go.

'I love you too, sweetheart,' he said gently. 'I think 'Tello was going to bring some chocolate cake. Do you think he will let you have some?'

Gemma beamed, completely won over. She ran to call Donatello on the internal phone. Luc grinned at his daughter's enthusiasm.

'Her stomach is alarmingly bribable,' he commented. 'I hope no young man discovers this when she's sixteen!'

Ellen laughed. 'It's a long time off,' she said, her mind racing through those future years, filled with school and parties, trips abroad, picnics and walks and celebrations together...

'Ellen!'

'Mmm?' She blushed. Luc had been saying something and she hadn't heard a word! 'Sorry. Day-dreaming!' she said breathily, her eyes dancing with silver lights.

'I said,' he repeated, 'that I've booked for us to have dinner at Le Gavroche, then I thought we'd go on to Annabel's.'

'Wonderful!' she cried. A proper date! 'Will this do?' she asked anxiously, indicating her dress.

Luc's eyes told her it would. 'It's wicked,' he said in a very satisfactory growl. 'You'll stop the traffic.'

'That'll please the pedestrians,' she said smugly.

He gave a little mocking smile. 'You won't stop me, though.'

'Oh, good!' she enthused, with a roguish wink.

True to his word, Luc could hardly keep his hands off her in the taxi, and she wondered if she'd arrive with her seams intact. Vibrant with elation, she swung into the famed restaurant with the intention of enjoying every sensual second of the food, and Luc's obvious eagerness to rush her home and seduce her.

When they walked onto the dance floor at the club later, he hauled her into his body as if he never wanted to be parted from her ever again. His mouth was in her hair, kissing her ear, moving to her neck, and she clung to him in a happy daze. This was perfection. The best day ever.

'Let's go back,' he whispered harshly. 'I don't think I can wait any longer. If you don't say yes, I swear I'll drag you outside and take you against the nearest wall!'

She felt like liquid beneath his hands. Dizzy with love, she could do no more than nod. In the taxi, he fell on her again and kissed her breathless. His energy transferred to her, firing her body till she felt that she could run a marathon and not be tired.

Throwing money carelessly at the driver, he raced with her hand in hand up the hotel steps, leaping them two by two and dashing through the doors and into the lift under the astonished eyes of the night porter. Once the lift doors had closed, he boldly slid off her briefs and tormented her with his touch till she nearly erupted with longing.

It was a long while before he hit the penthouse button for the lift to start its journey, and by then she was swaying in his arms, her leg sliding up and down the outside of his thigh and her mind and body and emotions completely intoxicated by his insistent and outrageous caresses.

Before entering the suite, they straightened their clothes and tried to quieten their breathing. Luc spoke briefly in a low, confiding tone to a strangely tense Donatello while Ellen, flushed and hardly aware of what she did, managed to find her way to her room. She heard Luc saying goodbye to his PA, then he made his check on the sleeping Gemma.

Ellen faced the door, her eyes bright. He came in and she saw he'd removed his jacket and loosened his tie. Without looking at her, he stumbled over and clumsily unzipped her dress.

And then, while she stood there trembling, he lifted her in the air. As if she knew what he wanted, she wrapped her long bare legs around his waist and he let out a ragged groan, staggering back to the wall for support.

'I mean to ravish you,' he muttered thickly. 'So thoroughly that you'll never forget it for the rest of your life.'

She quivered at the longing in his voice, and, more than willing, she let him lift her onto him, pushing on his shoulders so that the movement was smooth and sweet and utterly irresistible.

She adored this man. Loved his passion, his hunger for her, the way he smiled, held her tightly, the way they'd chatted and laughed all evening as if they were old friends…

Friends, she thought, her head going back as the rhythm of their bodies quickened and her breasts became slicked with perspiration. Friends and lovers…

She cried out, half dying with pleasure. Her eyes were wet with tears, and when she rested her head against Luc's throat she discovered the taste of salt. Blearily she looked up and saw that his lashes glistened and there was a track of tears on his cheeks.

'Oh, Luc!' she murmured with a shaky sigh, nuzzling up in contentment.

But he had other ideas and bore her to the bed. Time and again he made love to her, coaxing her with an almost remorseless persistence till she begged for release. She began to lose all idea of reality, her whole mind and body and soul focused on the smell and taste and feel of him beneath her, above her, beside her...

He's showing me how badly he needs me, she thought in one rare, lucid moment. And then his arm was dragging her down to the carpet and her body sank to his...which was still virtually fully dressed.

She pulled back, startled. 'Luc!' she croaked in a weak protest.

But he had rolled her over, and he was pinning her outstretched arms to the floor while he slid down, down to where she still throbbed, still hungered with a deep and insatiable heat. From that moment she abandoned conscious thought and gave herself entirely to him...

Till they both lay exhausted and sleeping in bed, clinging together in the wreckage of the linen.

CHAPTER SIX

Luc crawled groggily from the bed at four in the morning, forcing his limbs to obey his will so that he could stumble away from the scene of his final betrayal.

He allowed himself no backward glance, no last lingering farewell. That would show weakness.

Brutally he shut his mind to what he'd done and allowed the icy coldness of the shower to do the double job of punishing and waking him up at the same time.

God! He looked terrible! Haunted eyes, razor-sharp cheekbones, a thick stubble...

With shaking hands he managed to give himself a reasonable wet-shave and then he dressed, his movements becoming slower and his limbs heavier every second, as if they were trying to prevent him from carrying out his revenge.

But she deserved this. She had harmed his child. She had seen his wealth and envied and coveted it—and him too, because he was part of the package. He'd been aware of the greedy light in her eyes when they'd walked into the hotel and later into the restaurant. There had been plenty of telltale remarks to indicate that she was still a material girl at heart.

Angrily he shrugged on his jacket. It wasn't surprising. She was living in penury, it seemed, and she'd been brought up in a cocoon of luxury. It was natural she'd want that again.

But not that he should provide it and be paid with her body in return.

His hands shook. He felt an urge to do something violent. To trash the room. Beat his fist against the wall.

But he did none of these things. Sick to the stomach, he picked up the bag which the faithful Donatello had packed while they were having dinner, and collected Gemma's bag too.

He stopped in the middle of his daughter's room. She slept with her bottom in the air as usual, and his heart somersaulted to see how vulnerable she seemed. All he wanted was to protect her and keep her from distress. He had to remember that, to keep it in the forefront of his mind. She had enough hang-ups. She didn't need a grasping hooker for a mother as well.

Bleakly he stared into space, reliving the past two days. It pained him to admit it, but Gemma had undoubtedly enjoyed herself. A small uncertainty wormed its way into his mind till he scowled ferociously and ruthlessly banished it. Giving a kiddie a good time wasn't difficult— and Gemma had never shown the slightest interest in her mother. There had been no cuddles, no affection, no loving glances from his daughter.

He'd done the right thing. Ellen would be a bad influence. His jaw clenched as a surge of dark emotions robbed him of breath and rational thought. The power she had over him was evil. No man should want a woman so badly that he thought of nothing else.

Luc balled his hands into fists, shaken by the ravages that Ellen had wrought on him. He burned with a terrible and confusing desire to hurt and caress her at the same time. It was a shocking, visceral feeling, and he loathed himself for being reduced to a seething mass of base reactions.

Sourness wallowed in his stomach. Staggering to the wash basin, he poured himself a glass of water and spent a few precious moments conquering his urge to eject the contents of his stomach right then and there.

Hell and damnation. The biter bit.

Wearily he trudged back to Gemma. This was it, then.

He bent down and stroked her hair, then turned her over gently.

'Come. *Andiamo*,' he encouraged, trying to get her pyjamas off.

Like a floppy doll, she complied, her eyes fluttering open and closing again. 'We are leaving,' he said quietly, doing up the buttons of her cardigan. 'Going home.' He frowned, realising he was speaking in English. *'Andiamo a casa,'* he said clearly.

Gemma's eyes flipped open in dismay. 'No!' she cried suddenly. 'No! *No, Papà!'*

'Hush, *silencio*!' Astounded by her reaction, his senses dulled by exhaustion and strain, he was unable to catch her when she slipped from his grasp and ran into the sitting room, screaming her head off. 'Gemma!' he growled in warning.

Ellen heard the commotion and sat bolt upright in bed. 'Oh, my God! Gemma!' she breathed. 'It's OK! I'm coming!' she yelled, grabbing a sheet and, with swift presence of mind, ripping the bedside lamp away from its socket as a weapon.

She hurled herself into the sitting room, only to skid to a halt. 'Luc!' she cried in surprise, letting the lamp drop to a chair.

He seemed to be rooted to the ground, staring helplessly at the hysterically sobbing Gemma across the dining table. Astonishingly, they were both dressed, and when Ellen checked the clock on the wall her eyes widened. It was four-thirty.

'Whatever is the matter?' she asked in amazement.

Ashen-faced, Luc spoke, his voice so low that she could hardly hear. 'She doesn't want to go.'

'Go?' she repeated stupidly.

'Home.'

Baffled, Ellen tried to make sense of this. Why should Gemma suddenly take it into her head to bother about going home, when there were several days to go yet?

'Why not?' she asked, thoroughly muddled now.

'I don't know!' Luc roared in desperation as his daughter's sobs grew louder. 'Perhaps I woke her too suddenly!'

Ellen recognised that hopelessness and despair which had made him shout and she excused his outburst. Things were bad. If Luc couldn't calm his daughter, no one could. Ellen racked her brains for an explanation of Gemma's bizarre behaviour. There must be an answer somewhere.

Judging by the tone in his voice, Luc was trying to persuade Gemma to be calm and listen to him. Ellen had identified those particular words—and the fact that Luc was talking about the plane.

'Is it the plane journey she's scared of?' Ellen offered helpfully.

Luc flung her a scalding look, as if she'd said something stupid. She felt suddenly afraid. Something was very wrong. Steadying her beating heart with the pressure of her hand, she studied Gemma carefully while the little girl sobbed and shook her head at everything her father said, edging away like a terrified animal whenever he attempted to get near her.

Ellen's heart chilled. This was rank terror. The fear stared out from Gemma's huge, wet-lashed eyes. It trembled in her small rosebud mouth. It shook her scrunched up little body unmercifully and Ellen felt like crying herself, a hot, prickling emotion balling in her throat. She swallowed hard.

'Gemma!' she cried loudly, cutting through Luc's pleadings. 'We have five more days. You go home on Thursday. *A casa giovedi*—'

Miserably the little girl pointed to the door, her lower lip jutting in angry accusation. Mystified, Ellen swung around and her body turned to ice. It took a moment for her brain to catch up.

Luggage. By the door. But they couldn't be going. Luc

and she were crazy about each other. She and Gemma were making friends.

A tear welled up in Ellen's eye and splashed onto her hand. It was a mistake. Someone had been playing a trick and unsettled Gemma. She tried to speak. Nothing came out but a strangled, choking sound.

As if worked by jerking strings, she swivelled around, swaying precariously. Dimly she heard Luc pleading, promising that he'd care for Gemma and he would protect her from whatever frightened her. Slowly this seemed to placate Gemma, and she hesitantly came towards Luc while he shook with tension.

Then the little girl ran the last few feet into his outstretched arms and he buried his head in her neck, his groan of heartfelt relief bringing emotional tears to Ellen's own eyes.

Luc couldn't believe what had happened. He'd imagined that Gemma had wanted to be with him wherever he went. It had never occurred to him that she wouldn't want to go home! Yet that had been the plan from the start. Three days in England, then back to Capri. What on earth was going on in that little head? He was appalled that he'd unwittingly upset her, when his whole intention had been to fall in with her wishes.

Holding the now relaxed child in his arms, he mentally unleashed new curses on Ellen for making his daughter so unpredictable in her emotions. Donatello had been sure that she disliked Ellen, and he had always valued his loyal friend's perceptive judgements. From now on he and Gemma would be together. His vow to make her feel secure had been brutally reinforced by her confused behaviour.

When he lifted his face and looked directly at her, Ellen ached at the change in him. The lines seemed deeply etched around his mouth, which had become a hard, grim line, and his entire expression was terrifyingly harsh and utterly implacable.

Their eyes met. His were dead. Hers were bleached with shock. For in that terrible split second she knew that there had been no mistake. They were leaving without saying goodbye.

Numbly she gazed back at him with huge, horror-filled eyes, as the implications of this hit her like a punch in the stomach and she let out an involuntary gasp of despair.

Yet somehow, despite her collapsed lungs, she snatched a breath and choked out the question which was drawing the life from her.

'You…you're going…today?'

'Now.'

'Oh, God,' she mumbled faintly, and crumpled into a pitiful heap on the floor.

'The suite's been paid for till midday. Leave before then.'

She tried to make sense of it all but her confused mind refused to focus on anything. Luc's white and tormented face swam into her vision as she fumbled for understanding.

'You said…I had a week!' she protested plaintively.

'I lied.'

Ellen recoiled. A part of her was refusing to believe what was happening. Why, why? hammered her thoughts, pounding away relentlessly.

Suddenly she found her voice. It was rusty, but serviceable. 'But…' she grated, and, paralysed with shock, she whispered 'Why?' in a tiny, desperate squeak.

Luc dragged in a harsh breath. 'Because I don't want Gemma hurt any more. Because she becomes a worse psychological mess every time she visits you. I'm convinced you have a bad effect on her stability—'

'She wanted me this time!' Ellen defended.

'Don't flatter yourself about that. It was the better of two evils. She had a choice: to be at home without me, or to be here with you. She chose the latter, knowing that at least I'd be there for her in the evenings. This time I was prepared to let her have what she wanted. I knew I could keep a watch over what you did and how she was treated. But I'm not sending her out to you again. You rouse too many negative emotions in her and bring nothing but pain. It's over, Ellen. My child is too precious for you to play with or ignore as and when you please.'

His face showed no compassion as she started to digest what he was saying, his cold, almost robotic manner even worse than his earlier anger. He held the now sleeping Gemma closer, as if to keep her from evil, and Ellen trembled to see how much he hated her. She wanted to rail and rave and beat his chest with her fists. But that wouldn't get her anywhere at all.

'I could have made her happy this week!' she said in a low, pained voice as she struggled to keep her head. 'She might have become more settled once we'd—'

'Aren't you forgetting something?' he sneered. 'You wanted to dump her until you saw an opportunity to live the comfortable life again.' His face contorted. 'I know what you planned. You decided to use her as a stepping stone to me—and the life-style I could provide you with—'

'That's an absolute lie!' she gasped, wincing with horror.

'Is it? I wasn't the only one to come to that conclusion,' Luc said, scorn curling the high arch of his mouth. 'Donatello had your measure, too. He told me what you were doing, and warned me not to trust you.'

'You're both wrong!' she said heatedly. 'I was thrilled to be looking after Gemma—'

'You hide your feelings well, then,' he drawled.

She went quiet. Of course. She hadn't let him know how strongly she felt. Her caution was condemning her. Her shoulders collapsed in defeat. He wasn't going to listen. His mind was made up.

'You used Gemma for your own purposes,' Luc said

coldly. 'That's unforgivable. She needs security and continuity and I'd be failing as a father if I didn't give her that. You must understand that, Ellen! This is for Gemma's health! I have a right to put her first. This is the last time you'll see her.'

'Luc!' she muttered miserably, stunned by his icy composure. 'She's my baby! My little girl. You can't...' Something twisted his features. She choked on her tears, found strength flowing into her legs and jumped up. 'This isn't legal—!'

'It soon will be,' he bit, his whole body shaking with what she imagined must be suppressed anger. 'Once I report on your behaviour—'

'The art class?' Her eyes flared with pure rage. 'That's not fair, Luc!'

'Understand this,' he snapped. 'I'll do anything to protect my child and use any means I have to.'

'I'll fight you every inch of the way!' she declared in warning.

But her heart was cold. He had money and clever lawyers on his side. She was the absent parent and lived in another country. She had walked out on them when her child was helpless and in need. She was beaten, and knew it.

'Don't make it worse for yourself,' he said gruffly. 'Accept the situation and get on with your life.'

What life, without him, without her baby? she wondered, gripping her stomach to stop the awful, hollowing pains from making her cry out. Her hand raked shakily through her hair. Bitterness welled in her throat. Terrified of what he might say, but driven to ask, she made her dry, paralysed mouth work, doggedly licking her lips and chewing them into mobility.

'And...how do you explain what happened between us?' she ventured.

There was a long and terrible silence while he stared

at her without moving a muscle of his starkly pinched face.

'I'm not stupid, Ellen. I know that I was just the ticket to a Cartier watch of your own, beautiful designer clothes and the life-style you'd stupidly abandoned. You even admitted it.'

'Never!' she breathed, aghast.

'"Just be nice!"' he mocked in a silly, fawning voice. '"I'll do the rest! I know we'll learn to love one another...my life would be enriched!" You bet it would be! See, Ellen, the words were engraved on my heart because I knew that I'd be throwing them back at you sometime!'

'I—I was talking about Gemma!' she yelled in frustration.

'Like hell!'

'Luc, you've totally misunderstood everything I've said and done!' she cried, appalled by his obstinacy. He'd twisted everything that had happened. It was a nightmare. Her chin lifted. 'You can't deny one thing. We made love like there was no tomorrow—'

His eyebrow soared in contempt. 'We had sex,' he said succinctly. 'And there *was* to be no tomorrow as far as I was concerned.'

'No, Luc,' she flung, incapable of believing that her instincts could be so wrong. 'It was more than that and you damn well know it!'

'More? Yes, it was more!' he seethed through his teeth. 'It was my final revenge, my chosen way to get you right out of my system. And it was a lucky bonus that I enjoyed every moment of it!'

The room whirled, the sudden, violent passion of his words exploding their brutal message in her brain with terrible clarity. She reached out blindly for a chair and encountered his arm. He drew back as if she'd stabbed him and she kept going, half falling, and half collapsing onto the sofa, where she screwed herself into a tight ball of misery.

'I don't believe it! You planned it all…you actually *used* me!' she cried, almost choking on the words.

'Yes,' he retorted coldly. 'As you once used me till I no longer amused you. And I am now leaving you as you left me. That's my kind of street justice, Ellen. But remember that it was yours first.'

Her head snapped back, her neck hardly able to bear its weight any longer, and she emitted a long, keening moan. 'But I am totally innocent!' she whispered.

'The words "snow" and "hell" come to mind again,' he said with contempt.

And she knew it was all over because he was turning away and walking out with Gemma, just as he'd promised, and she was too numb to do anything more than sit there and let the tears blind her to their final departure.

The slam of the door cracked through her like a pistol shot. The two people she loved most in the world had gone. A few hours ago she'd been looking forwards to family life with them. And Luc had encouraged her in those beliefs so that she would suffer more keenly.

Oh, God, he was a swine! A vicious, heartless, calculating *rat*! Bristling with fury, she leapt to her feet, found the clothes she'd arrived in and doggedly, muttering and cursing, dragged them on her trembling body. Everything else she left. There would be no memories of this ghastly episode in her life.

And yet, helpless to stop herself, she had to have one last glimpse of Luc and Gemma. Leaning precariously out of the window, she could see the Bentley parked outside, its coachwork gleaming in the lamps fixed on the hotel's Georgian pillars. Luc's PA was loading bags into the boot and Gemma was running out alone…

Ellen drew in a gasp of breath, her eyes darkening with concern. Gemma had begun to pummel Donatello with her small fists! Luc suddenly emerged from the hotel, pushing his wallet into his jacket pocket and sweeping his hysterical daughter up.

Ellen watched them drive away and then drew back, pale with shock. The child was seriously disturbed. Her behaviour was so contrary that it didn't make sense. Unless...

She stifled her cry with her fist, refusing to think the unthinkable. Donatello loved Gemma. He couldn't be the one who...

'Oh, God!' she mumbled helplessly.

She had to do something. She couldn't ever rest until she knew what was frightening her daughter. She had to think. Dear heaven, her brain was in a mess! She strode up and down, trying to concentrate, but it was useless. Her mind just whirled and seethed with fractured thoughts and images and she gave up the struggle.

Her hands trembling with shock, she put the cash Luc had given to her in a clearly addressed envelope and handed it to the porter. Without knowing what she was doing, she began to walk. Gradually her steps quickened and suddenly she was running, oblivious of the darkness and the potential dangers lurking in the pre-dawn streets of London, running as if in some way she could escape her appalling fears for Gemma's safety.

Hampered by her shoes, she removed them and clutched them to her. Now her loping stride devoured the ground easily. The early-morning air cooled her burning face. On and on she ran, like a terrified animal, without thought of time or direction, ridding her body of anger and frustration and her injured sense of justice until her lungs finally gave out on her. All passion spent, all fury exhausted, she collapsed in a panting, gasping heap on a seat.

As she fought for breath, she realised she'd run all the way to St James's Park. Amazed at her stamina, she suddenly felt a strange calmness steal over her. And with that tranquillity came a crystal clarity of mind.

She had the power to do anything she wanted. *Any-thing*. To fight Luc, to assert her rights, to help Gemma.

He wouldn't get the better of her. She would not be his victim again.

And that meant she had to accept that Luc had never loved her. Ruthlessly she dashed away a tear which had seeped from the corner of her eye. There could be no time for self-pity when Gemma needed her so badly. Ellen bit her lip, controlling her own selfish emotions, knowing that her mourning for Luc would have to wait. This time she must not fail her daughter.

Gemma was terribly afraid of something—or someone—and Luc seemed incapable of seeing that. The solution was obvious. She would have to go to Capri.

With extraordinary composure, she stood up and walked all the way back to her flat, planning every step of her journey to Italy.

In the space of two days, she had taken temporary leave from her job, bought a cheap ticket to Naples with her meagre savings and was boarding the plane.

Making the arrangements had stopped her thinking about Luc's betrayal. Her only priority was to learn the truth about Gemma's strange behaviour and to deal with it.

A taxi driver with a death wish—and an ability, she thought angrily, to extract enough lire from her to have bought the taxi outright—dropped her outside the ferry terminal. Still, the kamikaze drive through the notorious Naples traffic jams seemed to have fired her up and crushed her nerves about the task ahead. Despite the vastness of the docks and the lack of signs, she managed to find her way to the departure point for the Capri jet boat. The last stage of her journey was about to begin.

The sun warmed her back while she waited for the passengers on the huge, high-speed launch to disembark. In a few moments she was slipping onto the ultra-smart boat with a crowd of noisy Italians, while the politely queuing American and European tourists looked on in alarm at such disorderly behaviour. She smiled wryly. When in Rome...

The beautiful boat skimmed along silently. People chatted excitedly, mobile phones rang and a man sang for sheer joy in a heartbreakingly liquid tenor voice. She relaxed, envying the warm affection displayed by the Italians, their capacity for happiness, for passion.

Perhaps, she mused, Luc had been out of place in England. Here the setting was so dramatic that a more extravagant, emotional response to life seemed appropriate.

And she longed to release her own emotions instead of keeping them locked within her chest. Longed to love uninhibitedly. To give her heart and to be loved in return. She sighed. It was too much to wish for. She would have to be content with knowing that Gemma's troubles were over.

In the summer haze, the vast Bay of Naples, the perfect cone of Vesuvius and the beautiful Amalfi coast grew a soft, misty blue. After just forty minutes, Ellen saw the small, luxuriantly green island of Capri begin to rise higher and higher from the delphinium-blue sea.

Her pulses raced. Eagerly she scanned the precipitous limestone cliffs and the slightly lower area of land in between. Flat-roofed eighteenth-century buildings huddled together on the top of this central hill. At its foot lay a harbour packed with boats, its waterfront a jumble of colourful houses sporting balconies and roof gardens.

It was incredibly beautiful. And she fell instantly in love with it.

'*Bellissima, si?*' murmured a voice beside her.

She smiled, glad she'd brought her sketchbook. 'Lovely,' she agreed, exchanging a friendly glance with the young, dark-eyed Italian.

The boat drew nearer to the shore. A huge lump came into her throat as she watched a school of dolphins frolicking beneath the sheer cliff.

'Tiberius. Roman emperor,' said the young man, directing her gaze to the top of the cliff. 'He lived there.'

'Lucky him,' she murmured wistfully.

'Threw his enemies off the rocks. One thousand feet to the sea!' exclaimed the man.

Ellen shuddered. They were a passionate and merciless lot out here! And then her fingers tightened on the rail. Perhaps, she thought daringly, remembering something that she'd considered before, perhaps…she *could* live here! If it had been good enough for Tiberius…!

Her eyes glistened. She stood in the bow, letting the air stream over her excited face as the boat manoeuvred up to the jetty.

It was a crazy idea, but not impossible in her current state of mind. She felt invincible. And she could do what she darn well liked! In an island four miles long, Luc could hardly keep her from seeing her child! Her lip quivered. It would be wonderful…

'Permit me.'

'Oh! Thank you!' she cried warmly to the young Italian, who had his hand outstretched for her case.

'You stay here? Holiday?' he asked, as they walked along the long jetty to the busy waterfront.

'Business,' she told him firmly, turning over the name of the lodging house in her pocket.

'I take you to your hotel?'

'No. Thank you,' she said, regaining possession of her case. The man took her hand in his and kissed it, managing to gaze passionately into her eyes at the same time. 'Goodbye,' she said pointedly.

He laughed. 'We will meet again,' he murmured, and, kissing his fingers to her, then giving her body a long, raking stare, he sauntered over to a nearby café.

Ellen wasn't bothered by his advances. Men were always doing that to her. Contentedly she sat on a bollard, swinging her long legs and tucking into her egg and cress sandwiches. Tourists bustled about, clambering on and off little boats to see the Blue Grotto, or boarding the high-speed launches to Naples, Ischia or Sorrento.

Idyllic. Her pulses quickened and she sat up tall, imagining herself here, acting as a guide, perhaps, or even a waitress in one of the hotels. Her eyes closed and she lifted her face to the sun in pleasure, the ever-present pain in her heart a little less intense than before.

In his office on the quay of Marina Grande, Luc was gripping the back of his chair in an effort to keep a lid on his temper. There she was again! Thick-skinned and arrogantly sure of the effect she had on men!

She'd swanned off his boat in a white suntop and short denim skirt, oozing sex appeal and sauntering along with a fawning lap dog in tow—who'd been dismissed the moment he'd served his purpose.

She seemed…serene. And that annoyed him. If she'd cared for Gemma or him at all, she would have been devastated by his rejection. Unless, he thought grimly, she believed that she could easily make him change his mind with one glance from her come-to-bed eyes and a wriggle of that heart-stopping body.

Well, she hadn't been up all night sorting Gemma's nightmares. That alone had convinced him that he must stick with his decision to simplify his daughter's life. He'd speak to Ellen in cold, concise words of one syllable so that she got the message once and for all.

Tired, angry, and shaken by Ellen's incredible pig-headedness, he stopped trying to gouge holes in his leather chair with his fingers, slipped on his cream jacket and headed for where she was sitting.

The sun was gilding the fine bones of her face and turning her hair to molten gold. Luc faltered, removing his sunglasses so that he could drink in her beauty. He loved the long arc of her neck, the way her jaw angled, the lushness of her parted lips. His body ached.

In stretching rapturously to the midday sun she had

caused her breasts to strain against the white cotton of her bootstrap top, and it was all he could do not to stride over and place his hands on her tiny waist, then slide them up over those marvellous curves.

He could feel her—in his fingers, his skin and in his loins. His mind was already playing tricks on his body, arousing him more than he could allow.

Instead of approaching her calmly then, he found himself raging at what she did to him. And he wondered if the only solution was to indulge his lust till it died. His pulses quickened. Then he frowned. Stupid idea. How could he do so and yet keep her from influencing Gemma?

Somehow, she never knew how, Ellen sensed that Luc was approaching, even though her eyes were still closed. She'd prepared herself for the possibility that she'd come across him at some stage, but hadn't expected to bump into him so soon.

There was only an imperceptible change in her breathing, but all her senses were alert and receptive to the force of Luc's energy field which had already intensified the air between them. Her skin tingled with electricity. It was the last reaction she wanted, and she fought to keep her nerve.

'You *are* a persistent little witch!'

He'd obviously intended her to be startled. To annoy him, she slowly opened one eye, looked at him for a second, and closed it. 'Mmm,' she agreed blandly.

She lowered her chin so that she could swallow without him noticing. He was furious, his eyes smouldering with rage, and yet her heart had leapt at the sight of him, looking devastatingly sophisticated in toffee-coloured trousers and shirt, and a pale cream tie and jacket. Sexy. Her pulses fluttered madly and she sucked in a breath to still them.

Luc muttered something that sounded rude. 'Don't you have any pride?' he asked coldly.

Opening her eyes now, she regarded him with a solemn expression. 'A lot,' she replied. 'To be perfectly frank, after what you did and said to me, I would never have wanted to come here if it hadn't been for Gemma.'

When he drew in a long and shaky breath, she saw how dark he looked around his eyes, as though he'd slept badly. And he seemed thinner. Her heart thudded anxiously. Was he ill? Did he have business worries? Or was he just worried that she'd corrupt his daughter?

'It's for Gemma's sake that I want you to turn right back and go home,' he said curtly. 'Ellen, I neither know nor care what you're doing here, but she's been impossible since we left London—'

'That's why I've come!' she cried, her own hostility forgotten. 'Something is frightening her, Luc—'

'Yes. It's the same pattern every time she sees you. You disturb her psychologically.'

Ellen rose and faced him with determination, her fists jammed into her waist. She flushed when his gaze trawled over her hips and began to wander insolently up her body, but she refused to let him put her off.

'I disagree. It's something else. I'll prove it. I'm going to find out what it is!' she said stubbornly. 'You can't stop me. I have a right to stay here if I want.'

For a few moments he frowned at her in frustration, and then he raked his fingers through his hair with a muttered expletive. 'Short of tying you up and throwing you on a boat, I can't stop you. But you risk hurting her.'

'No, Luc. If I believed that, I'd stay away. I've chanced all my savings and my job to come over here because I know what I saw: a terrified little girl who needs help. I intend to find out what's wrong. Now excuse me,' she said, touched nevertheless by the pained uncertainty in his face. He did love Gemma. It must be awful for him. 'I have to find where I'm staying.'

'Wait.'

His hand caught her arm and he looked deep into her eyes. She saw a strange vulnerability there and she softened. 'Don't let's fight over this. I'm very determined, Luc. You want her to be a happy and normal little girl, don't you?'

He let his hand drop and a steely light came into his eyes. 'Emotional blackmail now, Ellen?' he asked tightly.

She winced, pained by his obstinacy in seeing her as devious and amoral. 'For once,' she said in a hurt little voice, 'treat me like a human being and not a compulsive liar!'

Finding tears beginning to blind her eyes, she pushed roughly past him. And as she pulled the address of her accommodation from her pocket she found herself being detained again. Firmly he turned her around. Helpless in his grip, she scowled at the ground, reluctant to let him see that he'd made her miserable.

But he released his hold and touched her wet cheek. And then her heart stopped. His finger was pressing gently on her moist, sulky mouth and every bone in her body was weakening.

'You are upset,' he said gruffly.

Unable to answer, afraid she'd launch herself into his arms, she made do with a curt nod. Gently he brought out a cream silk handkerchief and dabbed at the tears on her cheeks, then wiped her eyes with great care.

'Better?' he murmured.

She fixed her gaze on the point where his tie dived beneath his jacket. 'Mmm.'

'I don't know what to do about you, Ellen.'

Hold me tight. Kiss me till I forget everything bad that has ever happened. And, above all, love me...

'Let me do what I want,' she pleaded instead, meeting his eyes at last.

There was a wry lift to the corner of his mouth. 'You always do,' he observed sardonically. Before she could protest, he held out his hand for the piece of paper she was holding. 'So. Where are you staying?' he asked in a resigned tone. 'I'll guide you there.'

'I'd rather be independent,' she replied quickly, preferring that he didn't know where she lodged.

'As you wish.'

His capitulation surprised her, but she smiled and said goodbye, and when he'd walked off she tossed up between queuing for the funicular cable railway, or treating herself to the luxury of a taxi. The taxi won. It whisked along a series of hairpin bends up the alarmingly steep hill and stopped almost immediately in a small taxi bay.

'Villa Maria?' she queried doubtfully, checking her map.

'No. There,' said the driver, with a vague wave of his arm. 'No cars in the town of Capri.'

'No...cars!'

'You walk.'

'How far?' she asked. At least her case had wheels!

The driver shrugged. 'Half-hour.'

Ellen blanched, but set off determinedly. A short distance beyond the taxi bay she saw Luc emerging from the funicular terminal. He gave her a mocking wave and she smiled cheerfully, as if she was enjoying herself, then ploughed on past a quaint little bell tower draped with purple bougainvillaea and into a beguiling square.

Ignoring the tempting tables and bright awnings of the cafés ranged around the little *piazza*, she checked her map and plunged into a narrow vaulted alley. The way quickly became very steep and cobbled, and then narrowed even more before deteriorating into a series of knee-wrecking steps. Every now and then a fresh flight of steps would plunge off down the hillside or ascend to the heights above, and Ellen had to check frequently to make sure she was heading in the right direction.

She felt hot and exhausted, but she kept going in the silence of the sticky afternoon because Luc was following her. If she'd been alone, she would have stopped and paused for breath, but he might have construed that as a weakness. And it suited her for him to believe she was tough and utterly unassailable.

'Are you lost, Ellen?' he enquired sympathetically, appearing at her elbow when she paused for the tenth time to study her map.

'No. Certainly not! I'm here,' she retorted, stabbing a finger at the place with absolute confidence.

'Impressive!' he admired. 'But you must be tired after your journey. Let me take your case.'

She was about to refuse when she saw how stupid she was being. Why should she pretend her ancestors were goats? And he was going to follow her, so he might as well be put to use! Gladly she surrendered her case to him.

'No one said the whole of this island was traffic-free and built on a vertical mountain!' she complained with a rueful smile.

He laughed. 'Most people only come for the day. They never find out. Aren't you the lucky one?!'

Ellen didn't speak. She was saving her breath. Without speaking they continued upwards, till Luc pointed to an opening on Ellen's left.

'Villa Maria, I think. Do you have ropes and crampons?'

Her heart sank when she peered through the gate. 'Left them on the Matterhorn!' she replied faintly.

No wonder he'd sounded amused. The villa seemed to be lurking somewhere at the top of a couple of hundred steps, which stretched up the hill with giddying monotony. Shattered at the thought of hauling herself up to cloud level, she leaned against the wall, her mind racing on in dismay.

Her accommodation was for room only. She would have to walk to the town every morning for breakfast and other meals. She would have to stagger down the hill every time she wanted to lurk near Gemma's school. And...she groaned. She'd have to climb all the way up again!

'Do you really want to stay here?' he asked.

'I'd prefer The Ritz, but this is what I've booked. Thanks for your help,' she said, keeping up a pretence of chirpiness. 'Bye.'

He gave her a faint smile, his eyes annoyingly hidden by sunglasses. 'I couldn't let you climb those steps unaided.'

And now that his departure was imminent she didn't want him to go. 'Neither could I,' she agreed, and he grinned.

Gratefully she let him put a steadying hand beneath her elbow and guide her up to the top, where she collapsed on a welcome seat and let her legs shake away unhindered.

'I'll sign you in, shall I?' he enquired, apparently little troubled by the climb.

Ellen nodded and handed over her passport, saving her breath for staying alive and vowing to start a strict exercise regime when she'd sorted Gemma out.

'It's rather primitive,' Luc said dubiously, when he emerged a few minutes later.

'All I could afford,' she replied, almost in a stupor, her hot face and slumped body showing her complete exhaustion.

He grunted, his face grim, and hurried down the steps without a farewell. Ellen watched him longingly. If only things were different between them. If only he didn't hate her. Feeling horribly dejected, she turned and walked very slowly into the villa. Whose surroundings depressed her even more.

Having discovered what time Gemma's school finished for the day, Ellen freshened up and felt a lot better. Eagerness made her hurry down the hill to the opposite side of Capri town. She easily found the school, which was perched on a plateau high above the sea. Five minutes after she arrived the children began to stream out, looking very sweet in their starched white pinafores. She stood beneath an oleander tree, hoping to remain inconspicuous, and anxiously waited for a glimpse of her daughter.

Out of the corner of her eye she became aware of Luc strolling along, greeting the arriving parents...and... Her heart sank. He'd seen her, and was heading straight for her, his mouth set in a grim line.

So she forestalled him with a friendly smile. 'Hi! Don't mind me. I'll fade into the background—'

'In those clothes?' He raised an angry and dissenting eyebrow.

After a brief check of her cropped lime top and short, washing-powder-white skirt, she had to admit that she wasn't exactly background material.

'I could find a bigger tree to conceal myself,' she said hastily.

He wasn't amused. 'I'd prefer it if you went. Don't cause trouble, Ellen. What are you intending to do?' he asked irritably. 'Say hello and goodbye? What do you think that's going to do to her? Don't you care about her at all? For God's sake, think of someone else other than yourself!'

Ellen bit her lip. This was going all wrong. 'I only wanted to see how she behaved when she thought no one was watching,' she explained. 'I didn't know you'd meet her. I thought Donatello might—or that she'd go home on her own because you live so near. The island seems safe—'

'It is. And 'Tello often does pick her up. But she prefers me to be here so I come when I can,' he said curtly, cutting into her babble. 'You know how easily she's disturbed—and yet you hang around here because you have some crazy idea that—'

'It's not crazy!' she defended. 'And I was going to hide,' she added haughtily.

'Well, do so before she shows up,' Luc snapped. 'You can't go on confusing her like this—'

'Mamma!'

Luc groaned and said something rude under his breath.

Guiltily, Ellen turned to see Gemma making a beeline for them. To Ellen's amazement, Gemma ignored Luc and came running to her, arms outstretched and with a face wreathed in delighted smiles. Ellen exchanged a startled glance with the astonished Luc and scooped her daughter up for a long and loving hug before putting her down again.

'I'm sorry, Luc, I didn't mean—' she began awkwardly, shaken by the pallor of his face.

'I don't believe this!' he whispered.

'She's pleased to see me!' Ellen's eyes were filled with tears. 'Now will you believe me?'

'I don't... I can't...' He frowned in bewilderment as Gemma sped off to a group of children. 'It doesn't make sense—'

'It does if you stop believing that Gemma hates me,' Ellen said quietly.

'I thought...' He looked apologetic. 'I was trying to do what was best for her,' he said shakily.

'I know. Maybe we can start again—'

Ellen's suggestion was interrupted by Gemma's excited squeals.

'Petra! Miranda!' Gemma cried.

'What's she saying, Luc?' Ellen asked as two girls, a little older than Gemma, came over and Gemma launched into a stream of joyful chatter.

'She's telling her friends that you are her mother.'

She frowned. 'That's it?' There must be more; Gemma's friends looked so odd—almost sullen and angry.

Luc nodded. And quietly he said, 'She wants you to walk back with us.'

'Oh!' She bit back her pleasure. 'How do you feel about that?' Ellen asked, hardly daring to believe what he was saying.

'Ambivalent.' But he gave her one of his crooked smiles, as if he was rather pleased.

She caught her breath. 'Me too!' She looked yearningly at Gemma's happy face and wanted to leap into the air. Starry-eyed, she left the decision to him. 'What should I do?'

'If I say no, I'll be the big, bad bear, won't I?'

'I'm afraid you will,' she said with a grin.

'Then you'd better come with us,' he said, and Ellen felt sure he was only pretending to be grudging. 'If it'll give Gemma and me a good night's sleep, it's worth it.'

'I could always dope your tea if you'd prefer,' she suggested drily.

'Smile sweetly at her friends and come along,' Luc growled, pushing his sunglasses more firmly on his nose.

She produced the sweet smile and obeyed, her expression radiant as Gemma took her hand and bounced about happily between the two of them, talking non-stop. Ellen did her best not to bounce along too. Luc really was glad she'd been accepted!

She also tried not to think that they looked like a proper family, but she failed. It was a wonderful moment.

Very soon they arrived at a pair of ornate wrought-iron gates. Beyond them she could see a path flanked by red and gold hibiscus bushes and a huge terraced garden which appeared to lead to the edge of the cliff. Just visible in the tropical vegetation, between banana trees and fan palms, was the long outline of a roof—presumably Luc's villa.

'Ellen,' Gemma said anxiously, when they paused at the entrance, 'you...my *mamma*?'

Emotion almost prevented Ellen from replying. Luc's

eyes seemed as pained as hers. Confused by his reaction, she crouched down and held both of Gemma's hot little hands.

'Yes, I am your *mamma*, darling. I have always been your *mamma* and I always will. *Sempre.* Always.'

Gemma's eyes grew enormous. 'And live with Gemma and Papà?' she said tremulously, with a child's ability to ask the most awkward question possible.

Ellen felt Luc stiffen. This was difficult territory. Trying to keep a cheerful smile on her face, even though she knew she was treading on eggshells, she said gently, 'I have somewhere to live. Up there, in the Villa—'

Gemma snatched her hands away from Ellen's and burst into tears. She flung open the gate so violently that it smashed back against the hedge. Before Luc or Ellen could stop her, she was running down the path, her sobs carrying back to them in the silent afternoon air.

Luc looked agonised, as if his hopes had been dashed. 'You see what happens whenever you turn up! You confuse her! You haven't thought this through at all. It won't work, Ellen!' Wearily he set off after his daughter. And over his shoulder he flung, 'You'd better stay away! From both of us!'

CHAPTER SEVEN

SHAKEN and upset, Ellen sat down on the wall by the villa, wishing she'd handled the situation with more skill. She should have known that Gemma would jump to conclusions. Poor little scrap. Like most children, she wanted her parents to be together...

Glumly she acknowledged that maybe Luc was right and that she was adding to Gemma's distress...and his. He'd seemed so pleased to have her around, and then that one remark had upset Gemma and ruined everything.

She concentrated hard. Somewhere in the mass of information she possessed lay the key to Gemma's peculiar behaviour.

It was clear that she wanted a mother. And she wanted her friends to see she had one too. Perhaps that was it, she thought. Gemma felt different, and like most children she only wanted to be normal, with both parents living at home and doing boring parenty things.

Her first task would be to find out if this was so. Then she and Luc could talk to Gemma and draw out the truth. But, she promised herself, she would observe more discreetly in future. And she'd avoid Luc like the plague.

Over the next few days she managed to conceal herself successfully outside the school. Each time, Donatello collected Gemma, bending to kiss her on both cheeks, admiring the drawings or models she carried, and hoisting her onto his broad shoulders while she clung happily to his smooth, dark head. Nothing odd there, unless it was Donatello's familiarity.

But her earlier fears about Luc's PA had vanished. She'd seen plenty of signs to know that his affectionate

displays weren't at all unusual. Donatello was only ex-
pressing his love for Gemma.

Ellen had noticed that children here were chucked on
the chin, stroked, kissed and teased by waiters and shop-
keepers, friends and relations alike. The kiddies showed
off their designer clothes, toted designer bags larger than
they were and tended to be admired unstintingly.

It had been one of her pleasures to watch the endless
parade in the evenings, as parents brought out their children and proudly put them on show in the small square.
Donatello was in the clear.

Avoiding Luc proved to be more difficult than she'd
imagined. It seemed he dined out every night in Capri
town. Hunting for somewhere inexpensive to eat each
night, she kept coming across him, either strolling into
one of the dozens of restaurants scattered around the little
square and the medieval streets beyond, or sitting at a
table in La Piazzetta. And he was always with a woman.

Miss Ski Slope seemed to hang on his arm more frequently than Miss Caribbean Beach, but he wasn't averse
to escorting other women as well. They all sported
haughty cheekbones and endless legs and were beautiful,
chic and dressed in classic Italian style in elegant black
or taupe.

Briefly Ellen wished her hair was glossy and simply
cut in a timeless bob, instead of hugging her head in a
thick, curly cap. She wished she had expensive, under-
stated clothes instead of her cheap and cheerful gear. But,
she sighed, what if she had? Luc wouldn't treat her any
differently. To him she *was* cheap. And only occasionally
cheerful.

And yet it annoyed and upset her that he could enjoy
the company of other women. That his arm would occasionally slip around the shoulders of Miss Ski Slope, or
his hand would hover on the small of Miss Caribbean
Beach's back as they negotiated their way through the
busy square.

She despaired of her jealousy. It was something she realised she'd have to cope with if she did come to live in Capri. Her stomach lurched. How would she manage if she and Luc divorced and she kept bumping into him and his wife…and family?

Ellen went pale, her hands trembling as she pushed her plate of half-eaten pizza away. How would that scenario affect Gemma? She'd be more insecure than ever. Luc couldn't do that to his daughter!

And yet… Fumbling with the change in her purse, she paid the bill, alarmed at where her thoughts were taking her.

Gemma wanted a mother. Luc loved Gemma and it was likely that he was actively searching for a substitute one. Gemma would be thrilled. Her eyes widened in horror. He'd have other children. He loved them. Oh, God!

'*Signora?* You all right?' asked the waiter anxiously, when Ellen staggered to her feet.

'Yes!' She managed a smile, left a tip she couldn't afford and quickly stepped into the crowded Via Roma, wishing her imagination didn't run away with her so badly.

This evening, she decided, she needed a drink and the company of hundreds, rather than the isolation of her lodging house. Numbly she walked to the lively *piazzetta*. It was early—eight-thirty—and Luc dined late, like most Italians, so there'd be an hour and a half before he'd appear.

She found a table with a commanding view of the gently lit square and set about calming her agitated mind. Several men eyed her, some flirted, two even approached her, but she gave them her coldest dead stare, and they vanished in search of friendlier prey.

'Ah! Hello!'

Someone was lifting her hand and kissing it. Indignantly she pulled it away without looking up and made sure her wedding ring was on display. 'Goodbye.'

There was a laugh she recognised. The man who'd carried her luggage! He had pulled out a chair and was sitting down beside her and ordering a cognac before she could stop him. Married women presented no barrier to him, it seemed. She frowned.

'You are too beautiful to do that,' he murmured, his face very close to hers.

And then she wished she'd jumped up immediately and walked away, because Luc was passing close by with Miss Ski Slope, his dark eyes full of anger as he took in the situation and—as usual—jumped to the wrong conclusion.

Ellen stared miserably after him. This couldn't go on, she thought a few moments later, thumping her way up the hill to the Villa Maria. She had to stop caring about him and wanting him to think well of her.

It didn't matter. There was no hope for her and she was stupid to even wish there might be. All she could do was find a way to live near her daughter and help Gemma—and herself!—to accept that she and Luc would never be together.

That night she lay awake in the tiny, bare room, convincing herself that she could live near Luc and not mind how many women he dated. After an hour, she gave up. She would mind. She loved him; it was as simple as that.

Sentimentally she went over everything he'd said and done since they'd spoken on the phone, recalling every detail, every gesture. And something odd happened. Whenever she saw his face it had a certain look about it. His eyes held a hidden message which she couldn't ignore. And there was his body language...

She sat up, her heart thudding loudly at an extraordinary thought which kept popping into her mind. He did care. He cared very much.

She racked her brain for proof. He'd desired her, that was for sure. Whenever he'd touched her there'd been an amazing charge of electricity between them—and that meant there was something special which pulled them together, no matter what he said, however coldly he looked at her sometimes.

Carefully she recalled each occasion they'd met recently. He'd often been angry. Could that have been pure jealousy? It seemed possible—even from that moment he'd shouted at her on the phone because he'd thought Cyril—*Cyril!*—had been her lover. Surely he'd overreacted, even if he had been worried about her morals because of Gemma?

Her hand went to her mouth. There'd always been a strong undercurrent between them. She knew that he'd been drawn to her as much as she'd been drawn to him. There had been moments of tenderness and yearning. She couldn't be mistaken on that.

And yet he'd resisted her and taken his revenge because he believed she was selfish and would poison Gemma's mind.

Ellen became very still. If this was true, if she could prove her innocence—and if she could heal Gemma's emotional wounds—then he'd be free of his prejudice and he'd be able to admit to his own feelings. She smiled wryly. So many 'ifs'!

Her breath shortened with tension when she remembered something she'd read a long time ago. Apathy was the opposite of love, not hate. Hate was a distortion of love. And Luc felt passionately about her; she knew that.

She stared into the darkness, her head spinning with hope. She had a chance. This was what her instincts were telling her. Almost at once, a coldness seized her spine. Supposing she was wrong?

She'd be humiliated again…and yet that seemed better than the alternative: never to know if she'd been right, never to have tried to win him back and always to watch him sauntering around Capri with a beautiful woman tottering beside him, gazing into his eyes…

'Damn it!' she muttered decisively, her eyes blazing with battle. 'He does love me! I know it!'

Much too agitated to sleep, despite her attempts, she finally slipped out of bed and washed, before dressing in a pair of old jeans and a simple T-shirt. It was six o'clock.

She walked down to the Punta Tragara and gazed out at the Faraglioni: three extraordinarily beautiful pinnacles of dazzling white limestone rising sheer from the black sea.

As she gazed at them in the silent beauty of the Mediterranean dawn, she promised herself that she would do everything in her power to bring about her own happiness, Luc's and Gemma's.

Feeling dizzy with excitement, she sat on a bench and watched the sun rise. Later, after a hot croissant and coffee in a nearby café, she ambled along, exploring a path bordered by walls foaming with purple and red bougainvillaea, blue morning glory, honeysuckle and jasmine. Capri was stunning. An enchanting mixture of sophistication and wild beauty. And she meant to live here with the people she loved.

The sound of children's laughter made her turn in surprise, and she realised she must be somewhere below Gemma's school. On an impulse she hurried towards the sounds.

For a while she remained partially concealed by a house wall and watched the children with an affectionate smile. She was about to turn away when she saw Donatello arrive by the gate with Gemma. He kissed her goodbye. Ellen frowned to see how tightly Gemma clung to him, though he led her firmly to the school gate, gave her a gentle push and left.

Ellen held her breath. Her daughter clung onto the bars of the gate as if reluctant to go in. Misery was etched on her little face. Then something happened which turned Ellen to stone.

Petra and Miranda ran up and started yelling at

Gemma. They seemed to be taunting her. And then one of them punched her hard in the stomach.

Oh, my God! she thought in horror. They're bullying her!

Ellen erupted with rage, racing towards the children, grabbing Gemma and protecting her with her own rigid and furious body while she yelled angrily at the two startled little girls.

'Don't you dare hurt my child!' she cried, white with distress, completely forgetting that neither of them would understand. 'How could you do this? She's smaller than you, you bullies! Leave her alone! If you ever dare...'

The girls had run off, crying. Ellen subsided a little and turned her attention to Gemma, cuddling her and stroking her hair tenderly. 'It's OK, darling. It's OK. There. Hush. It won't happen again. We'll see your teacher,' she said, shaking like a leaf.

And she knew why she'd reacted so fiercely. Tears began to stream down her face, mingling with Gemma's. She'd suffered years of bullying herself. And now her daughter was suffering too. It was too awful to bear.

'Go home,' mumbled Gemma into her shirt.

'Yes,' Ellen said with a sympathetic sniff, deciding that Luc must deal with this. Her Italian wasn't up to it. And she lifted the child into her arms, perching her on her hip. 'Let's find your *papà*,' she said into the mass of blonde curls, and Gemma nodded and buried her head in Ellen's shoulder, her small arms nearly throttling her.

Near to tears again, Ellen stumbled along the pretty little lane to Luc's villa and boldly let herself in.

'Luc!' she yelled frantically. 'Luc, are you there?!'

Reading the morning papers on the terrace, Luc heard Ellen's voice and jumped up in amazement. Now what? Would she never leave him alone? He stormed into the hall, ready for a tough confrontation.

'What the—?' He glared, infuriated that she should be holding Gemma in her arms. The child should be in school! 'Put her down at once!' he ordered. 'What the hell do you think you're doing?'

'Rescuing her!' To his astonishment, Ellen stalked into his drawing room and sat down, nursing Gemma on her lap. 'I've made a discovery,' she said in a strange, excited voice. But he saw that she'd been crying and her eyes were bright with tears. And her hands trembled uncontrollably.

'What?' he asked grudgingly, torn between grabbing Gemma and stroking Ellen's furrowed brow.

'Gemma's being bullied. Talk to her. Ask her all about it. And then you must go to the school and tell them that it must be stopped!' Ellen cried hysterically.

Luc stared. 'Bullied?' he said, feeling his throat seizing up in horror.

'By two little girls. Petra and Miranda.' He watched Ellen's shaky fingers smoothing Gemma's hair in a gentle, rhythmic fashion but he was still too stunned to move. 'I saw them taunt her—I think it was something about me. I heard the word "mother".' Ellen lifted her head up high and fixed him with one of her direct, accusing stares, her eyes welling with tears. 'Find out what they said!' she insisted. 'They p-punched her in the stomach,' she said tremulously. 'I think they've hurt her before. She had a bruise on her back—'

'Oh, God!' he whispered, appalled. 'Gemma. Gemma, *carita*…'

He sank to the floor and his child stumbled over to him, encouraged by Ellen's helping hands. Tenderly he held his daughter's hot little body close and cursed himself for being so blind.

'There were all the signs,' he said huskily, the evidence running through his mind with alarming clarity. 'She had a stomach ache every morning before school. She preferred England to staying here and going to school.' He drew in a ragged breath. 'When…when I told her that we were leaving England and returning to Capri—'

'She had hysterics,' Ellen finished shakily.

He squeezed his eyes shut. 'God, I've been so stupid!' he muttered in anguish.

Gemma kissed him again and again, as if she was forgiving him. But he couldn't forgive himself.

'What kind of father am I? I'm supposed to protect her from all harm,' he said hoarsely. 'And I let her down!'

'I think,' Ellen ventured, 'that you were certain her erratic behaviour was something to do with me and that I unsettled and confused her.'

Luc wiped Gemma's tear-stained face, appalled by his refusal to see beyond his nose. Yes. Ellen was right. He'd been so sure that she lay at the bottom of Gemma's troubles that he hadn't stopped to consider anything else. His poor baby. How could he ever forgive himself?

'Tell me about those naughty girls,' he said quietly to Gemma.

'I'll go,' Ellen whispered.

She looked dreadful. For a moment he thought it was because she'd witnessed her child's distress. Then he remembered her terrible stories of when she was bullied at school, and he realised that Ellen was finding this very hard to cope with.

'Stay,' he said gently. 'I think she needs you. And you need me.'

Her startled look and grateful nod said it all. She was reliving her torment at the hands of a set of vicious little snobs. Feeling the anger roaring through his body, he gritted his teeth and prompted Gemma to tell her story.

She seemed more concerned about her mother's tears as he translated snatches of information into English for Ellen's benefit.

'No, Mamma!' protested Gemma, slipping from his lap.

She gave touching little pats of sympathy to Ellen's knees, and Luc had to swallow hard before he could speak. He felt proud that his daughter could think of someone else at such a time. And seeing Gemma show love towards Ellen caught at his heart.

Seeing that Ellen's distress bothered Gemma, he decided to explain. 'Ellen was bullied,' he told his daughter in Italian, his voice gentle and understanding. 'She had a bad time. The girls at school teased her because she was different from them. She knows what it's been like for you. She knows better than I do.'

'I am sorry,' Gemma said to her mother in halting English.

His eyes met Ellen's. 'I'm sorry that you of all people had to be the one who found out,' he said to her. 'I'd have given anything to have shielded you from witnessing this.'

To his surprise, a slow and gentle smile spread across her face. On an irresistible impulse, he went over and sat next to Ellen, taking her hand in his and patting it like a fool. Gemma clambered onto Ellen's lap and stroked her soothingly.

They sat there for a long time, talking everything through. Sometimes Gemma would come out with a new and forgotten story of harassment, which always related to the fact that she didn't have a mother. She was the only one in the whole school whose mother had never shown up for plays, fiestas or school functions, let alone taken her to school each day.

He knew how much it must hurt Ellen to be reminded of her desertion. And, even though she had created the situation, he could feel nothing but compassion for her. It was clear that she really cared for Gemma now, and it plainly hurt her very deeply to know that their daughter had suffered so much.

'I'm so sorry,' Ellen whispered lovingly to Gemma. And Luc quietly translated when she continued with, 'I know how frightened you were. Any time you thought they might come around a corner and point at you and laugh at you and hurt you. It was something you thought about all the time, didn't you? And I expect they told you to keep quiet or something dreadful would happen.'

Luc felt so grateful to her. She could articulate Gemma's fears and was able to show that someone had shared them. The two seemed very close. Two pairs of grey eyes gazing solemnly at one another. Gentle smiles being exchanged. His hand tightened around Ellen's as Gemma's lids began to droop.

'Lay her on the sofa,' he said softly. 'Let her sleep. She's had such bad nights lately she must be very tired.'

'You'll go to the school?' Ellen said anxiously, after sliding Gemma off her lap.

'Oh, yes.' He frowned, his anger resurfacing as he thought of the damage done to both Gemma and Ellen. 'In a moment. Come into the next room so we don't disturb her. We can hear if she wakes.'

Beneath his hand he could feel her arm still trembling. When they reached the library he tilted her chin and looked at her carefully. Her lashes were appealingly spiky and there was a touching little quiver in her lower lip.

'I'll go to the school later. You're very upset. I don't want to leave you. Or Gemma.'

'I'm OK,' she said shakily.

'Not if your pulses are anything to go by,' he said abruptly, feeling how rapidly they were beating.

Unaccountably she blushed. 'I'm just a bit ragged round the edges,' she said in brave dismissal.

He had to get away before he leant over and kissed her. He couldn't believe that his lust should surface even at this highly unsuitable moment. Ellen was recovering from an emotional shock. His daughter was sleeping off the release of her trauma.

And yet, he thought grimly, wandering around the room and pretending to show a ridiculous interest in a flowering clivia, all he could think of were his own primitive urges.

'I don't know how to thank you,' he said, sounding tense and stilted.

'I don't need thanks,' she said gently. 'Knowing that Gemma will be all right is my best possible reward.'

'I've wronged you.' He frowned, wondering why this conversation should be so damn difficult. 'I misjudged you and your motives.'

'Yes,' she said equably, and he smiled ruefully to himself at her painful honesty.

He heard the soft whisper of her footfall and knew she was coming towards him. Then he felt her put a hand on his arm and he remained stiff, fighting back the longing to turn and press his mouth to her soft pink lips.

'Gemma did badly want a mother,' she pointed out.

'Every woman here under the age of eighty has been given the once-over for that post,' he answered wryly, thinking of Gemma's intense campaign to get him fixed up with a woman.

Ellen walked away before she let out a wail of misery. She felt as if he'd punched her in the stomach. He was telling her that almost any woman would do. Well, she thought angrily, any woman would *not* do! She had prior claim on the job. And on him.

Her eyes narrowed as severe doubts threatened the happiness she'd felt now that Gemma's troubles were being resolved. Luc seemed so edgy with her. He didn't want to look at her, let alone gaze into her eyes. Was that the behaviour of a man who unknowingly loved her? People in love touched one another often. They kept glancing at one another. But Luc was avoiding her.

A great sadness sat like a lump in the centre of her chest. She wanted Luc to love her as an equal, to be his friend as well as her lover. She wanted them to trust one another. But how could he do that, believing what he did about her?

And she couldn't solve the problem by telling him that she'd left him because she'd had clinical depression. She couldn't do that to him right at this moment. He already felt dreadfully guilty that he hadn't been aware of the bullying. No, the revelation about her illness must come later. Until then, he'd justifiably despise her.

She stood by the window, her eyes fixed somewhere in the mid-distance, where the sea sparkled and danced in the sun. 'Gemma wants me around,' she said levelly. 'I intend to stay. I don't know how I'll do it, but I am going to live here on Capri.'

There was a stifled mutter from Luc. 'In the Villa Maria?'

Her mouth pinched in as she realised how appalled he was. He didn't want her around! Her confidence wavered even more, and then she clenched her teeth and ploughed on, refusing to be swayed from her goal.

'I hope I can find somewhere better. I need a job so that I can support myself, perhaps work in a shop—'

'But, Ellen, do you know the cost of living on this island?'

'I've window-shopped—and realised that's about all I'd ever do here,' she said ruefully. 'It seems everyone's making money hand over fist.'

'No. The costs are astronomical. Think about it, Ellen. Virtually everything has to be brought in by boat. Food, drink, clothes, furniture, building materials... It all has to be shifted by luggage trolleys. Even building rubble has to be packed in small crates a man can carry. It's a vast, logistical exercise living here and we have to pay for it.'

'Not everyone's wealthy! Your maids don't get a fortune, I bet,' she protested.

'More than the going rate,' Luc replied. 'That's not the point. You're imagining some rosy future where you finish work and spend time with Gemma. Haven't you noticed that the shops stay open till nine-thirty at night? It's a non-starter, Ellen! One of your mad schemes—'

'I'll do it because I want it badly!' she cried passionately, whirling around in exasperation. 'I know it won't

be easy, but I must live near her, Luc. I want to form a
bond with her and I can't do that hundreds of miles away,
you must see that!'

He didn't comment, as she'd hoped. He didn't say that
he'd love that, or that she could stay with him, or even
that Gemma would be pleased. Instead, he moved around
the room, taking books off the shelves and rearranging
them. And she couldn't stand it any longer.

'Why don't you go to see the school?' she suggested
in a hard, flat tone. 'I'll stay while Gemma sleeps. We
must talk to her, Luc. Tell her how it is with us.'

'And...how is it with us?' he enquired with maddening
calmness.

She felt tempted to tell him she loved him. Her body
screamed with tension as she brought it under strict control.

'You tell me!' she said, throwing the ball back in his
court. And their eyes clashed. She recoiled at the fierceness of his stare, her lips parting in dismay.

'You want to know?' he asked huskily, a dangerous
glint now in his dark eyes. He began to walk slowly towards her. 'You want me to say it?'

She shrank back in alarm, her hand going to her dry
mouth. 'Luc,' she said nervously. 'We don't have to be
enemies.'

He kept coming. She backed up to the bookcase and
flattened herself against it. He didn't love her. His eyes
were full of anger and desire.

She'd made a terrible mistake.

'Enemies or lovers, Ellen,' he growled. 'You choose.'

'Why does it have to be like that?' she asked jerkily.

'I don't know!' he grated. 'Only that it does. I want
never to see you again...' She let out a low moan. His
thumb touched her mouth and through its gentle probing
she could feel the extreme tension running right through
his body. 'Or to have you in my bed whenever I want.

That's how I feel about you, Ellen. Do what you like with that information.'

And he spun on his heel and walked out.

She sat in the silence of the library, shaken to the core by Luc's declaration. What a choice he'd left her! To ignore one another, or to use each other for sexual release!

Ellen's jaw clenched. There was no tenderness in his heart for her. She'd misread lust for love. Anger for passion. So much for her instincts. She'd wanted him to care so badly that she'd imagined telltale signs where none had existed. Only a fiery, volcanic passion.

And that just wasn't enough.

She was still sitting there when he returned. Her heart felt empty. All her hopes had been dashed. Listlessly she looked up, her eyes devouring his taut, energy-packed body.

She must tell him she would make her own way in life and he could go to hell. Summoning up strength to move, she followed him into the sitting room where Gemma still slept.

'Everything all right?' she asked shakily, working herself up to a final showdown.

He straightened, keeping his back to her. 'Yes.'

'Then I'll go,' she said, with equal curtness. 'But first—'

'You're not going. You have to stay here!'

'You know I can't!' she snapped, glaring at him when he turned around. His face was grey and yet simmering with anger, and she felt a twinge of sympathy for the teachers and Petra and Miranda. It must have been one hell of a confrontation. 'I want you to explain to Gemma that I must live on my own—but that I love her. Say—'

'I'll tell her nothing. You have to stay!' Luc's eyes blazed into hers, meeting her defiance with a fierce obstinacy. 'I told them at the school that you would be living here!'

Ellen's jaw dropped open. 'What?'

'I had to,' he muttered. 'I talked to the headteacher and those two girls. I began to explain the situation and saw in their sly little eyes that they'd continue to persecute Gemma if they knew you weren't living with us as Gemma's proper mother. So I said you were.'

'You *didn't*!' she cried in horror. 'You know I can't live here!' Her neck began to feel hot. It was out of the question. She and Luc couldn't stay in the same house and keep their hands off each other! 'You'll have to go back and tell them you made a mistake—and make those wretched children understand that—'

'They're looking for a victim and that victim is our child! Don't you care about that?'

'Of course I care!' she said, white-faced.

'You have to do this!' he insisted. 'For Gemma! She wants you here. Hasn't she gone through enough?'

'Now who's using emotional blackmail!' she cried in despair, unable to bear the thought of Gemma going through hell again.

'I am,' he said grimly. 'If that's what makes you see sense. Pretend everything is normal, can't you? Let her settle down, have a month or two of normality—'

'It won't be in the least bit normal!' she fumed.

'We have to make it appear as if it is!'

'I'm not holding your hand and kissing you at the school gate for anyone's benefit!' she spat.

'Who asked you to?'

Ellen lowered her eyes in embarrassment. It had been the first thing she'd thought of. No. The second. The first had been that Luc would almost certainly come to her room if she slept one night under his roof.

'Oh, you mean appear married...as in *not* talking to each other!' she said waspishly.

Luc glared. 'All you have to do is to be here. Collect or deliver Gemma sometimes. You can have rooms in the east wing. You can be as independent as you like—but be around for breakfast and when she comes home. Dammit, Ellen, you know you owe it to her!'

Her nostrils flared with her indrawn breath. He'd hit a raw nerve. Close to weeping, she stared back at his impassioned face and knew that she couldn't refuse. Her departure when Gemma was tiny had left a scar on them all which would never heal.

Subdued, she put her hands over her face then slowly let them drop to her sides. 'For…a month?' she asked shakily.

'Till she's stable. You say you care about her. Show it!'

She winced. He had the power to hurt her more than anyone she knew. 'Oh, God!' she whispered painfully.

He paused, his eyes unreadable as he watched her wilting figure. 'I had to do it, Ellen. I had no choice.'

She heaved a huge sigh. He'd fight the world for his Gemma. 'I suppose so,' she said defeatedly, and sat down, her legs suddenly weak at the appalling thought of keeping Luc at arm's length for the foreseeable future.

CHAPTER EIGHT

SHE had moved in that same day, with Gemma dancing and singing and generally getting under her feet every inch of the way. There was no doubting, thought Ellen now, in relief, that she had become a totally different little girl. Gone were the scowls, the ready tantrums and tears. In their place was a happy, sunny-natured child who seemed eager to do anything for anyone.

It was that which kept her from packing her bags and leaving. Luc kept snapping at her whenever Gemma wasn't around, and there was a terrible tension in the air every evening. Fortunately he left immediately after breakfast, and Ellen was able to take Gemma to school and play the role she'd always longed for, that of a normal, boring, have-you-got-your-lunchbox mother.

Today Luc had phoned during the day, and asked her to join him for a drink on the terrace in the evening. Unusually, he was late, and she'd had to put Gemma to bed herself—not that either of them had minded too much because it was a delicious novelty.

Nervously she waited in her room, from where she could see the gate. A young man wheeled in a sack trolley full of exotic white flowers for the house, to supplement those from the garden. The two maids hurried out, chattering happily. Finally Donatello appeared—and then Luc.

She frowned. They seemed to be arguing heatedly. Luc's PA actually flung his hands up in the air, as if in rejection of Luc's argument, and stormed off. She leaned into the fluttering white curtains and watched the raw emotions on Luc's face. He seemed very upset.

She twitched the swirling skirt of her pale blue dress so that it lay snugly on her hips, and hurried down to the terrace. He was waiting there, a drink in his hand and a frown creasing his smooth brow.

'I saw you with Donatello,' she ventured. 'You two haven't fallen out, have you?'

He gave her a swift, unreadable look. 'I've sent him on a trip to England. He wasn't keen,' he said, in the kind of tone that prohibited further questioning. He took a sip of wine. 'I have found a part-time job for you.'

Her eyes opened wide in surprise. 'That's wonderful, Luc! Thank you! What is it? When do I start?'

'Tomorrow morning. You'll be dogsbody for the owner of the Vesuvia Jet Line.' A corner of his mouth twitched. 'He needs someone to shout at.'

She smiled. 'I hope he has a sense of humour! I'm just as likely to shout back! Tell me about him.'

Luc shrugged. 'Married, one child. Dragged himself up from nothing, owns five boats and a trans-Europe courier and haulage business.'

'Wow! Are you sure I can work with such a dynamo? My Italian is pretty basic—'

'Most people on Capri learn English, French and German as a matter of course. He's fluent in four languages,' Luc said briskly. 'Your hours are nine to twelve, which'll give you time to take Gemma to school. Some days you'll be asked to work from three to seven-thirty as well.'

'Fine.' She beamed. She would have financial independence. 'I'll be able to earn some money at last.'

He turned strangely veiled eyes to her. 'Yes. Without taking your clothes off,' he commented sourly.

'Let's hope so!' she said, intending that as a joke.

Luc merely scowled and she sighed, realising she'd put her foot in it again. He had a serious problem with his sense of humour nowadays.

'I'm having dinner out this evening,' he told her curtly. 'So I'll say goodnight.'

Ellen's face fell. She'd spent ages getting ready and had looked forward to being with him. Someone else was to have that pleasure. 'I'm going out on the town, too,' she informed him on impulse.

She'd already discovered that Luc's cook slept in the room next to Gemma's and loved babysitting. Why be miserable indoors alone when she could be miserable outside and watch other people have fun?

'Just remember your position,' Luc warned. 'You are my wife. You will not dine alone with a man.'

'And you?' she said sweetly, although her eyes betrayed her anger. 'Is it conventional for you, a married man, to dine with a woman who is not your wife?'

'I'm eating alone,' he said, much to her surprise.

It was ridiculous, she thought later, flinging caution to the wind and opting for a proper restaurant meal. A married couple, both dining in solitary state somewhere in a town big enough to walk around in fifteen minutes! Apart from the hilly bits, she amended.

Her brief amusement soon vanished. Stabbing a king prawn with her fork, she reflected that this couldn't go on. People would talk about their odd marriage and the talk would get back to Gemma and her friends. She'd have to make more of an effort to play the part, hard though that would be.

She did a lot of thinking that evening. It seemed ironic that she had—apparently—all she wanted. She was living on Capri, with a job, and therefore would soon have money in her pocket. Gemma was happy and she and Luc were together.

The one drawback was that their relationship was a sham. And she didn't know how long she could keep it up before it broke her heart for the second time in her life. She shuddered, remembering what had happened before.

The trauma of Gemma's birth had triggered her depression, but she'd been emotionally and physically weakened by the state of her marriage.

A coldness numbed her body. She never wanted to feel so helpless and suicidal again. If she was to get through this unscathed, then she'd have to put a barrier between herself and Luc. If she didn't, she could be facing years of illness. There must be no more loving. No wishing. When they weren't in the public eye, she'd treat him like a distant cousin with bubonic plague.

Her eyes closed with the pain of facing the truth: that she and Luc had never had a chance. He'd known that but she'd refused to admit it. But now she must, for her own survival.

Luc appeared late for breakfast, snatching a cup of coffee just as she and Gemma were leaving. Ellen didn't even look at him, and she felt proud of that small but significant achievement.

'Sorry,' he said to them both. 'Overslept. I'll walk you to the office, Ellen.'

'Right.'

Tired from lack of sleep—another night spent tossing and turning—she allowed herself a cursory glance. He didn't look refreshed at all. Even the snappy pale grey linen suit and pale pink shirt couldn't conceal his weariness, and he was particularly monosyllabic when they accompanied Gemma to school. Still, Gemma did enough talking for everyone, and much to Ellen's relief she ran off happily to her classmates.

For the short time while they waved goodbye, Luc draped his arm around Ellen. Remaining stiff beneath its welcome weight, she allowed its presence there, knowing it was just for show. It was therefore no surprise to her that as soon as they'd walked around the corner he removed his hand and maintained a careful distance thereafter.

Following a path lined with fragrant jasmine and ole-ander, they passed an old man playing a clapping game with a toddler on a seat. Luc smiled and stopped to talk to them, his hand caressing the child as he spoke. Ellen remained cool and aloof, trying not to be charmed by the sight, but her heart turned over at Luc's soft smile.

It seemed that fate was working against her. When they moved on, their quick strides brought them close on the heels of a grey-haired maid who was pushing a buggy and singing softly to her charge. Luc greeted her enthu-siastically and she turned in delight, kissing him on both cheeks and clearly extolling the virtues of the infant.

Of course Luc had to crouch down on his haunches and amuse the child. Of course he had to look infuriat-ingly tender and murmur in his wretchedly liquid voice!

Ellen walked on, pretending to admire the view of the aquamarine sea. Luc caught her up after a moment and rested a hand on her arm in brief apology. He didn't no-tice how rigid she was, or that her muscles had contracted at his touch.

'Wife of my gardener,' he said by way of explanation. 'She works for a friend of mine, Lucia de Vecchi.'

'Sweet child,' she said in a low voice.

He smiled. 'An angel.'

She made no comment. This gentle, affectionate Luc was slowly eating into her heart. She wished he'd be hard and brutal, so she could hate him. It was difficult to keep her emotions in check when he showed such a genuine capacity for human love.

'You're very quiet,' he said suddenly.

'Thinking of my job. Bit nervous,' she muttered.

'His bark's worse than his bite.'

'I'd rather he didn't do either!' she said, conjuring up a small smile.

'I think—I hope—you'll enjoy the experience.'

Luc waved to a friend. As they entered the busy street which led to the *piazza*, it seemed that he was constantly greeted, slapped on the back and kissed. It was, she thought crossly, something of a King's progress.

People liked him. He liked them. And never was he more appealing than when he stopped by a puffing middle-aged woman struggling up the incline to the *piazza* and courteously offered her his arm.

He and the woman even paused to admire a pair of exorbitantly expensive shoes in the window of a stylish boutique. Luc was encouraging the woman to buy them, even though they had skyscraper heels.

Ellen was about to remonstrate with him, and point out that the woman's feet were bad enough without sticking her on top of scarlet stilts, when she saw how flattered and excited the woman looked.

Bright and bubbling, instead of slumped and frowning, the middle-aged lady wagged her finger at him playfully and started back up the hill as if turbo-charged. Ellen realised that Luc's flattery had raised the spirits of the life-weary woman, who had long ago stopped seeing herself as glamorous or frivolous.

Silenced by the warmth and depth of his charm, Ellen waited while Luc chatted to a group of porters. She studied him carefully while he talked animatedly, asking after their children. He was a mystery, she thought, with an enormous capacity for loving and an equally frightening ability to hate.

'Is there anyone here you don't know?' Ellen asked with a sigh when they finally entered the square.

He stopped and held her firmly, forcing her to look him in the eyes. 'Only you.'

Behind him the clock on the bell tower rang out its tinny chimes. The newsagent sang as he tidied his papers and brought his bounding dog under control. There was a cacophony of chatter and the sound of mobiles ringing all around but he continued to gaze at her intently.

And she felt a deep sense of isolation amid the friendliness and warmth surrounding her. She wanted to belong to his world. To be part of him. To be welcomed and liked, greeted, kissed. Capri was small and intimate and essentially Italian, and she knew she would never be accepted if she froze Luc out. And yet she must.

Another loss, she thought sadly. She would be an outsider here.

'I'll be late,' she said primly. 'The Dynamo will shout at me.'

'I think he probably will,' Luc agreed with an amused smile, and guided her to the funicular railway which would take them down the steep hill.

'I can't think of a nicer way to get to work,' she ruminated, as it set off down the almost vertical track. 'Walking along a flower-edged path without a car in sight, then whooshing down to the harbour.'

'You like Capri?'

'Tremendously.'

He pressed her hand. When she looked at him in surprise, he smiled. 'It's a big step, changing your country of residence. I'd be concerned if you hated it here and were only staying for Gemma's sake.'

The unmoving sea shone as if it had been polished. In the distance, a hydrofoil approached from Sorrento under a cornflower-blue sky. Huge magenta trusses of bougainvillaea spilled over ancient Saracen walls and far below fast, expensive yachts bobbed, waiting for their owners to step in and sail off to elegant resorts.

Ellen drew in a contented breath. She had more than most people ever dreamed of. 'Thanks for making it easy for me. I'll try not to make waves.'

He gave a short laugh. 'I'm drowning already!' he joked.

'As if!'

Happily she allowed herself to be jostled with the rest of the commuters, who were all attempting to get off at the same time. Ellen hardly noticed.

This was lovely. If she couldn't be Luc's lover, then

they could be friends. His attitude delighted her, and she walked arm in arm with him along the quayside in high spirits, while he pointed out local characters and points of interest along the way.

'That's your dynamo's office,' he said, pointing ahead. 'Eighteenth century. Rather fine.'

Ellen hurried towards it with him, feeling excited and nervous as they walked beneath the rose-covered arch. The building had been carefully restored, with high airy rooms, and cool arches and tinkling fountains in the central courtyard. Huge palm and banana trees soared from deep flowerbeds foaming with bright geraniums, and smartly dressed men and women bustled back and forth, acknowledging Luc with smiles and handshakes.

'It's stunning! Terribly lavish!' she whispered, worried that he'd leant on this dynamo to give her a job. She'd feel horribly obliged to be perfection itself. Why hadn't she found something for herself? Then, if she was sacked, she wouldn't feel so ashamed...

'In here.'

Luc opened a door and showed her into a room with a commanding view of the harbour. 'Fabulous!' she cried in awe. 'This desk is antique, isn't it?' Luc nodded, clearly amused by her delight as she toured the large office, running her hands over the raw silk sofa and feeling the satin finish on a huge rosewood chest. 'Oil paintings, silks, *lavish* drinks cabinet—this man knows how to live!' she whispered.

'He certainly does.'

'When will he be here?'

'He is.'

'Oh. Am I to wait for him?'

He gave her an odd look. 'He'll make his presence known.'

She nodded and cautiously settled herself in a damask-covered chair, trying to look demure and calm. Trying to *be* calm. Luc wandered around, flipping papers here, reading a letter there.

'Luc! You can't do that! Supposing he comes in?' she hissed in horror.

He smiled and threw a switch on the answer-machine, listening to the first message and making notes.

'I don't believe what you're doing! What on earth...?' She saw his raised eyebrow, his confident air, the... Oh, why, she thought, grinding her teeth, hadn't she noticed the name on the darn desk? 'You trickster! This is your office!' she wailed.

'Very good,' he murmured. 'Now open the post or I'll start shouting.'

She did nothing of the sort. 'You're the Dynamo!' she groaned faintly.

He held out a letter-opener. 'Correct. I'm switched on. What about you? Get opening.'

Almost without realising, she started to slit the envelopes he handed over, her mind not fully in gear. 'I—I had no idea you were so...'

'Rich?' he supplied, slipping off his jacket and draping it around the back of a leather chair.

'Successful,' she corrected.

'You remember I sent money to my mother every week?'

She nodded, her fingers deftly busy as they extracted his correspondence, smoothed it out and laid it in a neat pile.

It had been a problem. They hadn't had enough to feed themselves and yet he'd insisted on sending money home.

'I remember,' she said fervently.

'She saved it, every penny. When Gemma and I left England for Naples, she bankrolled me. With that, and the sale of the truck I had, I bought shares in a small boat and took tourists on trips along the coast. Gradually I built up this business.' He hesitated. 'Before we continue, I think you should know that I've bought your father out.'

'*What?*'

'It's been my ambition ever since he sacked me,' he said, his eyes as hard as anthracite. She shivered. 'That was the reason I had to fly to England at short notice. He was ripe for the plucking.'

She frowned. 'You mean…he was in trouble?'

'He overreached himself. Donatello handled all the negotiations. It wasn't till the last moment that your father knew I was involved and by then it was too late.'

'I see.' Ellen didn't know how she felt about this. Perhaps…compassion for her proud father. 'Is…is he all right?' she asked tentatively, surprised by the sudden rush of concern. She cared for him, she realised, really cared! 'Poor darling, he was so proud of his achievements. Losing the business must have been a bitter blow.'

'It was. I rang your mother shortly after. It seems he was like a lost child. And she sounded as if she was enjoying her new role, selling the mansion and buying a new house, telling him what, where and how they were going to live.'

'I must ring,' she said, suddenly fired with the desire to heal the old wounds.

'Big of you.'

'They wanted the best for me,' she told him gently.

'And I wasn't.'

'No! I mean…I meant that they only saw things from their point of view, not mine.'

'People always think of themselves. Few are generous enough to sacrifice their own needs for others,' he said quietly.

He meant her. One day, she promised herself, she'd tell him what had happened. Very soon.

'My parents—all right, my father,' she amended, 'was right in a way. We should have waited, Luc. We shouldn't have let them push us into marriage when we had no money and no knowledge of one another.'

Luc smiled. 'Ironic that he'd been a lorry driver and was determined his daughter shouldn't marry one!'

'But his rejection drove your ambition,' Ellen pointed out. 'You were determined to show him that we hadn't made a mistake.'

'I wanted the best for *my* family. I think I worked too hard, didn't I, Ellen?' he asked quietly.

'Heaven help me, you were as proud as Father!' she replied with a wry smile. 'You felt you had so much to prove. And you did,' she said, with a wave of her hand around the room.

He'd taken risks which had terrified her, remortgaging their tiny house when her father had sacked him so that he could purchase a truck and go into the haulage business himself.

'But I'm easing up.' He was by the door now, closing it and checking a large wall calendar there. 'I'm downshifting so that I can spend more time with Gemma.'

'I'm relieved to hear it. She needs you.' She eyed him helplessly. 'You know I can't work here,' she said with great reluctance. The office and its surroundings were wonderful. Pity about the employer. She loved him too much to spend the whole day with him—and to keep that love a secret for long.

He leaned against the wall and folded his arms in a gesture of intransigence. 'It's here, or nowhere at all.'

'Don't spoil it,' she said sadly. 'We were getting on so well—'

'So let's continue to do so.'

'No! Luc, we absolutely can't work together—'

'Why?'

That softly spoken query absolutely stumped her. She could hardly say because she'd be unable to stand the sexual tension day after day.

'Never mind that! You tell me why I have to work here!' she demanded irritably.

The black bars of his brows drew together. Swiftly,

decisively, he came over and took a letter and the opener from her hand.

'Because,' he replied, 'I am not having any other man spending several hours a day with you.'

Dry-mouthed, she wilted at the glow in his dark, smouldering eyes. 'W-why not?' she stammered stupidly.

'You don't need to ask that,' he said quietly. 'You know the answer. Make me a coffee, please.'

She swept the empty envelopes into the bin. Of course she did. He didn't trust her with anyone. Gloomily she checked the small espresso machine for water and switched it on, placing cups beneath the twin spouts. He thought she'd flirt with any available males. And that remark he'd made earlier about taking her clothes off was plainly a reference to her lack of inhibitions about making money.

'Don't you have a secretary to do this?' she muttered.

'Normally I do it myself. But since you're here—'

'Do you have a secretary?' she persisted, thinking of notepads and sitting on knees and blondes in tight skirts.

'Sure.' He smiled and flicked on his intercom. 'Toni? *Si, per favore.*'

Toni, she thought. Definitely a blonde. Long legs, big bosoms. She sucked her stomach in and tried to look fantastic.

'*Ciao*, Luc!'

Blond. Long legs... No bosoms. Male! Ellen grinned. 'Hello!' she said happily. 'I'm Ellen.'

'Maccari,' Luc supplied.

She slanted him a look. He was marking his territory again. 'I might be working here if I like it,' she told the beaming Toni, putting Luc in his place.

'Shall I show you around?'

'Please!' she said eagerly. She needed time away from Luc to think things over.

'Don't be long,' Luc warned, settling down at his desk

and looking genuinely preoccupied. 'I have errands for you.'

She grinned. Errands! He did mean to give her dogs-body jobs! Perhaps, she mused, they could be civilised about this. If he treated her as courteously as he treated friends and staff, then they'd get on brilliantly.

The cheerful Toni introduced her to every office and everyone in the building. She liked him a lot and pumped him for all she was worth, discovering that the dynamo was also a paragon, and, judging by Toni's unstinting admiration, was in danger of being placed on a pedestal for all to worship!

There was one snag. Miss Ski Slope turned out to be Luc's transport manager—her real name being Lucia de Vecchi. Chatting to Lucia, envying her ready smile and welcoming manner, Ellen decided then and there that she would work with Luc.

OK, she argued, strolling back to the office, there wasn't anything she could—or should—do to curb Luc's roving eye. And hands. She grimaced. But she wanted to know what was going on so she could be prepared for that day when he finally asked her for a divorce and began making plans for his second wedding.

'Your transport manager,' she said bluntly, when she returned. 'She's the one you took on holiday.'

He finished checking a column of figures. 'Jealous?' he enquired, fixing her with an interested stare.

That was too near the truth. She had to drop her gaze. 'Huh!'

He chuckled. 'Lucia de Vecchi is Donatello's married sister. That was her baby you saw this morning. We have dinner together sometimes—'

'I know,' she said grimly, before she could stop herself. 'Doesn't her husband mind?'

'He's dead. Cancer. Donatello and I take turns to amuse Lucia, to get her back into society again.'

'Oh. Sorry.'

'You're dying to ask me something else,' he said, amused.

'All right, I will!' Nothing venture, nothing gain. She had to know. 'The woman you went to the Caribbean with—'

'Donatello's other sister. One of five of them altogether.'

'Big family,' she observed sulkily. 'I suppose you take them all out to be even-handed.'

He laughed softly. 'Something like that. Remember that 'Tello is my closest friend. I think I told you that we grew up in Naples together—in the same tenement building in fact. Many's the time we were back to back in a street fight, fending off a rival gang. His sisters are my sisters. Their troubles are mine. I'm a kind of...friendly uncle, dishing out advice, wiping away tears, offering jobs and playing best man at weddings. Or,' he said more soberly, 'offering consolation at funerals.'

'Oh.'

'Is that all you can say?'

She nodded, her eyes huge with sorrow. He was kind and loving and generous to everyone except her.

'If you're working here,' he said gently, 'sort out those files. If not, close the door quietly on your way out.'

Her mouth twitched. She grabbed the files and shuffled them noisily. Luc ignored her and bent his head to his work, but she could see a smile fighting to emerge. And soon she was fully engrossed in the tasks he gave her, determined to prove that she was reliable and responsible and could do a good job.

Her morning went too quickly and so did the next. The rest of the week passed like lightning. There were awkward moments: tense silences when she and Luc accidentally brushed past one another, or when they were enclosed in his office for more than half an hour. It was difficult not to be sexually aware of a man like Luc. And he clearly found it hard not to be aware of her.

She, however, was so happy there that she was prepared to cope with these moments. To give Luc credit, he did his best to remain friendly but detached. Perhaps he knew she'd leave the minute he made a move on her. Whatever the reason, she was very grateful.

Luc had all the qualities Toni had claimed. As the days went by, she began to assess what had happened to break their marriage up. He'd been misguided, over-eager to provide well for her and the coming baby, but he hadn't been deliberately neglectful.

And...she'd never told him that she felt deserted and lonely. How had he been supposed to know that she wasn't behind him one hundred per cent of the way?

When she'd been ill, no one had known what was happening to her, not even the doctors. Pressure had been on both of them. She couldn't hold him to blame for being shocked and bewildered by her behaviour. Ellen sighed. It had been a mistake not to talk. She'd remember that in the future.

And that future seemed promising. Her surroundings and the working atmosphere couldn't be faulted. She liked everyone, and she and Luc strode to work each day talking nineteen to the dozen—which gave her a quiet, secret joy. And she was now included in the kisses and greetings from his friends and acquaintances, which meant she was beginning to feel very *loved*.

Even her parents had sounded warm and welcoming when she'd spoken to them. She'd promised to call in to see them and had glossed over her whereabouts, intending to explain when they were all together. It wouldn't do to alienate them with talk of Luc, just when there was a chance they could all be friends again.

As for Gemma...she was so different that she and Luc marvelled at the change in her. To Ellen's delight, she could now participate in all the things parents had to do, and it seemed that Gemma had totally accepted her. The two of them often sat together, drawing Luc, Maria, or anyone who would sit still long enough. Luc, of course, was impossible, and kept making funny faces which had them in stitches, but Ellen was thrilled with Gemma's progress—and the fun they were having together.

Dreamily she wandered home one day, after shopping for some new underwear. She bumped into Donatello, who'd returned from England two days earlier, and they walked back together.

'I have something for you,' he said, when they stopped by Luc's gate. 'I want to say I am sorry I have not welcomed you into Luc's life. This is a gift to say how I feel.'

Ellen took the small box with feelings of embarrassment. 'You didn't have to do this,' she said awkwardly. 'I understand you were protecting Luc from me. You're his friend. You should… Oh, 'Tello!' she cried in delight. 'It's lovely! But I can't—'

'Please accept it,' he said quickly, taking the silver spider brooch and pinning it to her dress. 'Wear it to show that you forgive me.'

Her face softened with smiles. She reached up and kissed him on the cheek, touched by his thought and by his diffidence. 'Thank you,' she said warmly. 'I will. See you tomorrow.'

He smiled back. 'Luc's invited me to dinner.'

'That's lovely!' she cried, and took his hand. 'Come on. They're having a swim.'

Everything—almost everything, she amended—was wonderful! Bursting with happiness, she led Luc's PA into the villa, eager to let Luc know that Donatello approved of her at last!

But something odd happened. Instead of welcoming her, Gemma went very quiet and clung to Luc. There were no hysterics, only a quiet trembling which pained Ellen more than any yells or tantrums.

Pacing up and down the drawing room while Donatello

tried to make polite conversation, Ellen prayed that the bullying hadn't started again.

Her head jerked up when Luc appeared, looking worried. 'You must speak to those girls again!' she said in a pained voice. 'They can't be allowed to upset Gemma—'

'It seemed,' mused Donatello thoughtfully, 'that she was afraid of you.'

Ellen paused. 'Yes. Perhaps they've been saying things about me. Luc, please do something! I won't have them ruin my relationship with my child!'

'I'll go now,' Luc said grimly. 'Don't worry,' he added encouragingly, when she continued to prowl around the room in agitation. 'I'll sort those kids out once and for all.' His soothing voice gentled. 'It's been good these past few days. I don't want that spoilt either.'

But spoilt it was. The two little girls, the school and Gemma herself denied there had been any bullying. Luc did everything in his power to get to the root of the trouble but nothing budged Gemma from her story.

She, Petra and Miranda were best friends. And everything pointed to the truth of that.

That night, Gemma's nightmares began again. Ellen listened to her daughter's cries and forced herself to stay in her room. But every nerve in her body was urging her to comfort her child. And when there was silence once more, she turned her face into her pillow and wept.

For the next two days, Gemma ignored Ellen. Trying to accept Luc's counsel of patience and a low profile, Ellen did her best not to take this personally. But she felt very low. If her child didn't want her after all, what on earth was she doing on this island?

Facing the unthinkable—leaving Capri, Gemma... Luc—she put down the papers she'd been checking for Luc in the office and suddenly began to cry.

'Ellen!' he muttered in concern. Gently he drew her into his arms. 'Don't. I know how it must feel. Be patient. She's confused about something—'

'B-but…if she doesn't want me…' Too upset to continue, she buried her face in his shoulder.

'She will,' he promised, holding her fiercely.

Her arms reached around his neck for comfort. Mournfully she mumbled, 'I was so ha-a-appy, Luc! And every time I'm happy, something comes to kick me in the teeth!'

'Hey!' Smiling, he stepped back a little and caught her chin in the cradle of his hand. 'No one's going to kick you in the teeth.' He paused, his eyes fixed on her trembling mouth. 'Oh, Ellen! You're irresistible!' he groaned. And very tentatively he proved that by kissing her.

She didn't pull away. At that moment she wanted all the loving and caring he could give. Her mouth opened beneath his and she twisted her hands in his thick, sleek hair.

The kiss deepened and became increasingly passionate. She knew she was breaking her promise to herself but she needed him. She wanted him, there and then. Slowly, utterly mesmerised, she watched while he undid the top button of her neat white shirt.

'I've wanted to do this for so long. Spending the day with you has been agonising. I've thought about this every night,' he breathed.

Weakly she pushed at his shoulders, but it was a feeble, token attempt to resist him. Every night! If only she'd known, she wouldn't have wasted her time counting so many maddeningly useless sheep!

And then she heard the chatter of a fax machine outside and dragged her senses back into her brain. This was no solution. It would only cause more problems.

'No,' she said firmly, straining away from him.

'Took you five buttons to protest,' he murmured, his finger exploring the swell of her breast.

'If you're suggesting—'

'Ellen,' he said urgently, kissing her throat. 'Let's be

practical. We're living together. We need each other. Why not enjoy one another?'

'Because—because...'

His dark head lowered, cutting off her floundering. And, as his mouth teased her uplifted nipple into a hard, throbbing peak, she despaired that she wanted him more than her own sanity.

Her body clung to his in an involuntary surrender, and he must have felt the softening of her tense muscles because he growled deep in his throat and raised his head to gaze intently into her eyes.

'You know I can't stay away from you,' he said shakily.

Lightly his mouth brushed her temple. She quivered when he stroked the nape of her neck and inhaled the perfume of her hair. When she remained silent and tense, he took her hand and kissed her fingers reverently. And then he touched her lips with his again, very gently, tasting the warm softness of her mouth.

She loved him so much. Her eyes closed in a wash of pleasure to be in his arms again. Slowly, kissing and murmuring endearments all the time, he pushed her back to the desk till its hard edge brought her to a halt. And then he bent her back, his mouth ravaging her throat and breasts while she whimpered her encouragement.

They were aware of nothing but one another. The raw, pulsating ache in Ellen's body was too compelling to deny, and Luc's gentleness became a savage urgency in response to the demand of her frantic hands and mouth.

'Ahem!'

They froze at the sound of an embarrassed masculine cough. Luc stared at her in bewilderment and then came to his senses, drawing her upright and placing her behind him.

'Donatello!' he said in relief. He gave a self-conscious laugh. 'Thank God it was you!'

Ellen hid behind Luc's broad back, wishing it hadn't

been anyone. Crimson with humiliation, she dragged her shirt into place, finding it impossible to do her buttons up because her fingers were shaking too much.

'...or I wouldn't have come. But I think you should see her,' he was saying stiffly.

Ellen wasn't paying much attention. She was trying to haul her body back to earth. And push a scrap of plastic into a neat hole. Buttons, she thought testily, were more trouble than they were worth.

Luc listened to Donatello, his mind refusing to hear what his friend was saying. Ellen wouldn't hurt Gemma!

'It's not true!' he cried, switching to Italian so that she couldn't understand.

'Luc, we've been together a long time. You know you can trust me,' Donatello said. 'I've talked to Gemma. I guarantee that when you see her she'll bear out what I'm saying. Ellen has frightened her. Perhaps unwittingly,' he admitted, 'but Maria can confirm that Ellen has been filling her head with stories about ghosts and witches, and now Gemma fears that monsters are waiting around every corner. She's absolutely petrified, Luc. Almost hyperventilating. Maria has called the doctor, she was so terrified of Gemma's mental condition.'

Anguish ripped through Luc's body. His poor baby! 'No. There's a mistake,' he whispered. This was the woman he'd almost made love to just now. She couldn't be that stupid, that unthinking.

'Go home,' urged Donatello. 'Take Ellen. See Gemma's reaction.'

He nodded numbly. His friend was wrong. Someone else had planted those stories, if stories there were.

'We're going home,' he said huskily, turning to Ellen.

She blushed, still fiddling with her buttons. 'We can't, Luc! We're supposed to be working!' she whispered.

'Here.' Quite controlled and detached now, knowing that his child needed him to be calm, he fastened them for her. 'It's an emergency. Donatello says Gemma has been sent home. What are you doing?' he finished irritably.

'Searching for my spider brooch. Oh, Luc, we must hurry! Can we take a taxi?'

He gave Donatello a quick glance. That wasn't the reaction of a woman out to ruin her daughter's emotions. 'Sure. Coming, 'Tello? I want you to be there.'

'So do I,' his friend replied grimly. 'So do I.'

It was only a short while later that he walked into the kitchen with Ellen and Donatello, whereupon Gemma twisted in Maria's arms, her face tear-stained, her huge eyes fixed on her mother in abject terror. He went cold to the bone.

'Sweetheart—!' Ellen cried, taking a faltering, bewildered step forward.

With a sob, Gemma fled upstairs, shouting something about a witch. 'Go to her!' he said in a choked voice to Maria.

It was true, then. God help Ellen. Ashen-faced, he faced the inevitable. She would have to go.

CHAPTER NINE

THE doctor arrived. Ellen waited in the kitchen, desperate to know what was wrong with her daughter.

'What's going on?' she begged Donatello. 'I haven't understood anything anyone's said—'

'You've frightened her,' he said brusquely. 'Told her stories about witches. She thinks you're a witch, Ellen.' He sat down across the table from her and leaned forwards. 'You'll have to go. Luc won't allow you to stay now.'

She stared at him open-mouthed. 'I haven't frightened her—'

'You damn well have!' roared Luc from the doorway. 'Where did you get that brooch, Ellen?'

'What?' she asked in bewilderment.

'God!' Luc strode over and tore it from her, ripping her shirt.

'Now just a minute—!'

'Sit down!' Luc's hand came down on her shoulder. 'It's a magic brooch, according to Gemma,' he ground out, his furious face close to hers. 'The sort witches wear. And God knows, I'm inclined to agree with her!'

Ellen's mind raced. And made a crucial connection. Donatello had given her that brooch…Gemma had been terrified of her before. The time Donatello had carried Gemma into the café, kicking and screaming. And Ellen had dismissed the silly impression that Gemma had looked at her as though she were a witch.

She tensed, all her faculties alert. This was Donatello's doing. She lifted her head high, appalled that someone

178

who loved Luc should be so devious and risk hurting his beloved child.

'Donatello gave the brooch to me,' she said, tremors of intense anger making her voice unsteady. 'I wouldn't dream of telling Gemma spooky stories. If you talk to her I think you'll find that Donatello is behind this—'

'That's it!' roared Luc, his temper exploding. 'You behave irresponsibly and frighten my child and then you put the blame on the man I trust above everyone—'

'I'm telling the truth!' she yelled.

'Truth?' he scathed. 'You don't know what the hell that is! Why would Donatello want to frighten Gemma? He loves her! He knows about children—a damn sight more than you do—'

'I wouldn't hurt her!' she protested in a horrified whisper.

'You have. By God, you have! I want you out of here. You've got an hour.' Contempt in every line of his face, he pulled out his wallet and threw a bundle of notes on the table. 'Find somewhere to stay tonight and then get off this island!'

Barely in control, he turned on his heel and stormed off up the stairs.

Shaking with emotion, Ellen stared at the money.

'Time to go,' murmured Donatello.

'Hell!' she raged suddenly. 'I won't let you do this to me! What do you have against me? What have I ever done to you?'

He looked her up and down without concealing his scorn. 'You are bad for Luc.'

She jerked her head up with pride. 'Oh, no, I'm not! I make him feel good!'

'Wrong.' Donatello leaned forwards, his loathing plain to see. 'When Gemma went to visit you, I saw that Luc hated it. I love him, Ellen. He is like my brother. I would do anything for him. And I had to help him to forget you.'

She gazed at him, appalled. 'So you filled Gemma's head with tales about me—as soon as she could understand what you were saying! You poisoned her mind against me years ago!' Ellen could hardly breathe. This was a terrible kind of love.

'I know it was wrong. I know it upset her,' he admitted in a low tone.

'Upset her?' she exploded. 'The situation was difficult enough for her, without you putting your oar in! How could you? You—' Emotion almost overtook her. All those years of misery and heartache... 'You ruined the relationship between Gemma and me! That's unforgivable, Donatello!'

'It had to be done; there was no other way!' he snapped. 'Luc was being torn apart. He had to cut you from his life. He would have done, but you had to come here! You discovered that Gemma was being bullied and Luc felt obliged to let you stay—'

'But you couldn't allow that, could you?' she said bitterly. 'You had to make my own child so petrified of me that Luc would throw me out—'

'Whereas,' came Luc's harsh, emotion-lashed growl from the door, 'Luc will be throwing *you* out, Donatello! How could you do this to me? You've almost ruined my *life*, don't you realise that?'

Ellen saw the PA's face collapse in horror when he turned and saw the unholy fury on Luc's face. In the midst of her relief, she felt pity for the man. He'd sought to blacken her name out of misguided loyalty to Luc and for no other reason, firmly believing that Luc was better off without her.

'Luc! I can explain! She's not good for you—!' Donatello gasped.

'Out!' Luc's eyes blazed with a frightening cold rage. 'Our friendship and everything we've been to one another prevents me from beating you to within an inch of your life. But don't presume any further. I want you off my land—and off the island within the hour. Oh, God, 'Tello!' he cried passionately. 'You of all people knew how I felt!'

'I couldn't bear to see you hurt,' the man mumbled.

'You can't turn him away, not after all the years you've been together,' Ellen said huskily.

'You'd plead for him?' Luc asked in amazement. 'You could forgive this man who destroyed your hopes of being a mother to Gemma? I'm damned if I could. You're strong, Ellen. And more compassionate than I am!'

She went over and put her hand on his arm. It was shaking with tension and she could feel the energy and rage surging within. 'He thought he was doing the right thing. He was wrong, and he must put things right with Gemma, but don't reject him, Luc. He's been a loyal friend to you. He loves Gemma—'

'And hates you.'

'Just leave the door open,' she urged. 'Please. For your own sake as well as his.'

Face taut with fury, he turned to Donatello. 'I suggest,' he said coldly, 'that you take yourself off for an extended holiday somewhere. I might have cooled down when you return. I might not. I guarantee nothing. You've betrayed my belief in you. I detest it when I discover I can't trust people close to me.'

Ellen watched Donatello's slumped figure slip from the room. She knew how he felt at that moment, and she felt sad that the wonderful and lasting friendship between the two men would never be the same again.

'I can hardly believe it,' Luc muttered. He straightened his shoulders. 'First I must put this right with Gemma,' he said quietly, his face showing deep lines of strain. 'And then we talk.' He caught her hand. 'I can only say how sorry I am for doubting you. I don't know how you'll ever forgive me.'

'The evidence was pretty damning. I thought...I

thought that I'd never see either of you again,' she said with a sniff.

Luc's hand caressed her head. 'I could murder that man for what he's done!' he growled.

'We can settle Gemma's mind. That's the most important thing.'

'I'll be a while with her. This needs tackling carefully. Why don't you have a long, relaxing bath?' he suggested.

Tenderly he kissed her. He seemed about to say something, but he checked himself and, with a choked mutter which she didn't catch, hurried off.

She must have slept in the bath, because the next thing she knew was the sound of knocking on the bedroom door.

'Just a minute!' she called in confusion, stepping from the freezing water. She wrapped a big fluffy towel around her and hurried to open the door. 'Gemma!' she cried in gentle delight. 'Oh, Gemma!'

The little girl hesitated, and then came forward and embraced Ellen.

'She wanted to say goodnight,' Luc said huskily.

Ellen felt her heart do somersaults of pure joy. 'Goodnight, my dearest darling,' she whispered. And, smiling when her daughter tugged shyly at her hand, she obediently went with her and listened while Luc read the bedtime story.

'All right, now?' Luc asked Gemma, caressing her forehead.

'I love you, Papà,' she cried, flinging her arms around his neck.

'I love you, darling,' he replied.

Gemma anxiously met Ellen's adoring eyes. 'I love you, Mamma,' she said, as if begging forgiveness.

Ellen leaned forwards for her hug. She held the sweetly smelling child and felt the tears start in her eyes. Gemma was hers again. And nothing would ever separate them.

'I love you, my dearest Gemma,' she whispered brokenly, overcome with emotion.

She and Luc left the room. She couldn't see. The tears were flowing down her cheeks unchecked, all the tensions of the years welling up.

Luc's arm came around her. 'You poor darling,' he said softly. 'You'd better dress. You're cold.' He rubbed her body as they made their way to her bedroom.

'W-w-what ab-bout you?' she sniffed, wiping her eyes with a corner of the towel. 'You must feel hurt and betrayed—'

'I do.' He sat down on the bed and drew her beside him.

She saw that he looked absolutely shattered. 'I'm so sorry,' she said feelingly.

'Donatello and I had one hell of a bond between us. It's finished.'

He put his hands to his face in despair. She brought his head to rest on her shoulder and stroked his hair in silence. And then she touched her lips to his scalp, aching for him, wishing she could ease his pain.

Suddenly, quite naturally, they were kissing: gentle, tender kisses which almost broke her heart with their hesitancy.

Luc moved back and took her hand. His finger traced the half moon of her thumb and the lines around its knuckle, and then he turned her hand over and kissed her palm. Without releasing her hand, he slid from the bed and knelt in front of her, his dark, molten eyes mesmerising her with their intensity.

'So much has happened between us,' he said thickly. 'But the past is finished. We've hurt one another. But I love you, Ellen. I've always loved you with more passion than is good for me. Donatello saw that. You even saw us arguing about it, outside the villa gate. That was when I told him I was going to make you fall in love with me all over again.'

Ellen gasped. He hung his head and Ellen, hardly daring to believe what he'd said, saw that his lashes were wet. 'What did he say, Luc?' she asked in astonishment.

'He was angry and said that I was a fool to be swayed by my loins,' Luc went on distractedly. 'He was convinced you were a worthless slut. I imagine that's why he stepped up his campaign. He couldn't bear you to take care of Gemma. Right from the moment we first met, when we were teenagers, he kept filling my head with things about you...and I listened. After a while I began to believe—'

'Perhaps he was jealous. Your friendship was everything to him,' she said gently. 'He worshipped you.'

Luc frowned. 'I know I don't deserve you, that—'

She placed a finger on his lips. 'You had every reason to mistrust me and to believe I was shallow and selfish. No, listen. Let me tell you.'

Tenderly she kissed his upturned face. And she told him of her illness and how terrified she'd been for Gemma's safety.

He listened in growing horror. His Ellen had needed him and he had been blind to the nightmare she was living day by day. She'd made the ultimate sacrifice and surrendered her child to his safekeeping.

What had he done? Yelled at her, reviled her, hated her...

If only she'd *told* him—yet she hadn't, *couldn't*, which meant he had been so impossible to talk to that she'd abandoned everything she'd loved.

No wonder she had despised him. He was an insensitive, mindless brute...

She was telling him she blamed herself for not saying how she felt, that she'd been scared and lonely, and feared she was losing her mind. The doctors hadn't known the extent of her illness, she was saying. Why should he?

And her hair. Dear God, she was telling him that her lovely hair had fallen out in handfuls! Unable to bear it any longer, he pulled away from her and staggered to his feet, his fists clenched as guilt and anger raged through his body.

She'd never consider living as his wife now. They'd have to live apart—and he'd suffer agonies every time he saw her...

'You must let me do something,' he said hoarsely, his brain thick and turgid so that he hardly knew what he was saying. She'd need financial help. Yes. 'Money...'

'I don't need your money, Luc.'

He ran his hand through his hair. 'What, then?' he asked, close to despair.

'Being your wife would do.'

He began to pace up and down furiously. 'Yes. That's it. Whatever you want. You can live here, in the main part of the house, and I'll move to the wing— Oh, God, Ellen, how can you ever forgive me?'

Ellen giggled. For an intelligent man, he could be really stupid sometimes!

'I don't have any choice,' she said patiently, breaking into his demented rambling. 'I love you. And I'm not tramping halfway around the house every night to make love to you.'

He stopped in mid-stride. 'What?'

She let the towel slip a little. 'Pay attention,' she said severely. 'I want some recompense for your inexcusable lack of common sense and your stubborn vendetta.'

His eyes filled with desire. She saw his mouth grow hungry. And then he snapped himself back into what he imagined she wanted: an obedient penitent.

'Yes, Ellen. Recompense. What can I do?'

How long before the penny dropped? She lay back on the bed, making sure that the towel rucked up around her thighs when she wriggled into place. 'Love me, you dolt!' she murmured.

There was a long silence. Ellen played with the edge

of the towel where it nestled over her breasts. She didn't
think either of them were breathing.

'As in...make love to me, or...' He cleared his husky
throat. 'Or as in *love* me?'

Her lashes seemed suddenly heavy when she looked
up at him. And her voice sounded slurred when she said,
'I demand both as my right.'

Luc shuddered. She stretched out her hand and he came
to her.

His mouth closed over hers.

'Lovely,' she mumbled.

'There's more,' he said throatily, pulling the towel
away.

'Oh, *good*!' she murmured with a wicked grin.

Makes
any time
special

Enjoy a romantic novel from
Mills & Boon®

Presents™ *Enchanted*™ *Temptation*.

Historical Romance™ *Medical Romance*™

MILLS & BOON®

A man for mum!

Mills & Boon® makes Mother's Day special by bringing you three new full-length novels by three of our most popular Mills & Boon authors:

Penny Jordan
Leigh Michaels
Vicki Lewis Thompson

On Sale 22nd January 1999

FREE

4 BOOKS
AND A SURPRISE GIFT!

We would like to take this opportunity to thank you for reading this Mills & Boon® book by offering you the chance to take FOUR more specially selected titles from the Presents™ series absolutely FREE! We're also making this offer to introduce you to the benefits of the Reader Service™—

★ FREE home delivery
★ FREE monthly Newsletter
★ FREE gifts and competitions
★ Exclusive Reader Service discounts
★ Books available before they're in the shops

Accepting these FREE books and gift places you under no obligation to buy; you may cancel at any time, even after receiving your free shipment. Simply complete your details below and return the entire page to the address below. *You don't even need a stamp!*

YES! Please send me 4 free Presents books and a surprise gift. I understand that unless you hear from me, I will receive 6 superb new titles every month for just £2.40 each, postage and packing free. I am under no obligation to purchase any books and may cancel my subscription at any time. The free books and gift will be mine to keep in any case.

P9EC

Ms/Mrs/Miss/Mr ....Initials...
BLOCK CAPITALS PLEASE

Surname...

Address...

....

....Postcode.......................................

Send this whole page to:
THE READER SERVICE, FREEPOST CN81, CROYDON, CR9 3WZ
(Eire readers please send coupon to: P.O. BOX 4546, DUBLIN 24.)

MILLS & BOON®

Makes any time special™

The Regency Collection

Mills & Boon® is delighted to bring back,
for a limited period, 12 of our favourite
Regency Romances for you to enjoy.

These special books will be available for
you to collect each month from May, and
with two full-length Historical Romance™
novels in each volume they are great
value at only £4.99.

Volume One available from 7th May